CHAMELEON

THE AWAKENING

MAGGIE LYNCH

Windtree
Press

https://windtreepress.com

Cover Artist: Christy Caughie of Gilded Heart Design

Publisher's Note: This is a work of fiction. Names, characters, places, and incidents are a product of the author's imagination. Locales and public names are sometimes used for atmospheric purposes. Any resemblance to actual people, living or dead, or to businesses, companies, events, institutions, or locales is completely coincidental.

Chameleon: The Awakening/ Maggie Lynch. -- 2nd ed.

ISBN EBOOK 978-1940064-00-0

ISBN PRINT BOOK 2nd Edition 978-1-947983-45-8

❀ Created with Vellum

For my cousins, Sarah and Krista.
May you always find the path which
vanquishes the darkness and moves you toward the light.
May magic remain with you forever.

ACKNOWLEDGMENTS

First, I must thank the Crit-Wits--Kristen, Gina, and Dawn--who first heard the idea for the Chameleon and helped me brainstorm plot points and form it into an actual story pitch. Second, my thanks go to Margie Lawson who critiqued the first 50 pages of this manuscript in its infancy. She taught me a great deal about tension, pacing, emotion through her critique. Her teaching took my writing to a completely different level of craft.

After the fifth draft of the first book, my wonderful beta readers provided valuable feedback in the next rounds of editing: Jim Lynch, Terri Reed, Michele Templer, Jerah Welborn, Clare Carter and Ellie Canning. Special thanks to Jerah, Clare, and Ellie who are voracious teen readers and gave me very valuable feedback on how it compared to other YA fantasy books they enjoyed.

Two people made the final difference in the formation not only of this book but of the entire series. Special thanks go to Elaura Rennie, who provided such immense insight as to structure that it helped me to create a new framework for the entire series. And to Mark Rennie, who provided the first conceptualization of the pitches for each of the subsequent books in the series. Without Elaura and Mark these books would be significantly less than they are today.

Writing a Fantasy series requires more world building and attention to details than other books I have written in the past. In the case of this specific series, it also required an overarching philosophy of cultural and religious beliefs, mythologies and ethics that fit the world. For this I could only rely on my own fortunate background and upbringing. From the moment of my birth my life was filled with unconditional love. My parents taught me how to seek the light even in times of tragedy. My siblings have always accepted me for myself, no matter what directions I wandered. Throughout my life, my parents and my siblings have brought different kinds of magic to me--the magic of wonder, the magic of knowing, and the magic of family loyalty.

Finally, no amount of words could ever be sufficient to express my thankfulness to my husband, who daily reinforces his love for me in ways that are indeed magical and enduring. It is not easy to understand the creative process of a storyteller. It is not easy to live in an environment where that process can be all encompassing and create days or weeks of forgetfulness about daily life. It is not easy to accept the vicissitudes of economics in publishing--never being sure if the next book will even make enough to buy groceries. Yet he has endured. More than that, my husband has encouraged me to continue writing my stories whether they ever bring material wealth or not. That is a special and rare gift of love. I am indeed fortunate and I thank all of you.

PROLOGUE

Sunlight filtered through the fog and softly lit a small circle in front of the Life Tree. The stately oak was diminished by the redwoods towering above the eight-foot Nakani as he carried Fia in his furry arms and set her feet upon the lush lichen at its base.

Fia let out a low moan and stretched against the life tree, her arms hugging the bark as the labor carried her into and through the pain. The tree infused her with some relief, but not so much as to take the pain away entirely.

She smiled up at Nakani as new tears brimmed in her eyes. "You know they will kill you for this."

"Only if they find me," Nakani answered, his large hands massaging her arms and shoulders.

"You must promise me," she said for the tenth time. "Promise to take the babe to Bliant. She lives beyond the barrier of singing trees in the land of Agnoses, near the Klamath River.

"I will not promise," Nakani shook his massive head as he

stepped behind her and rubbed her belly. "You will guide the babe yourself. I will not allow you to die."

Fia relaxed against him, snuggling into the dark auburn hair that covered his body from head to foot. When she had chosen Nakani, she knew she was going against all the rules by loving a member of the Quatcho. She knew they would have to live apart from both Quatcho and Mazikeen. However, she didn't know she would be banned forever from using Mazikeen magic. Even the dragons would not overrule the Mazikeen queen in her proclamation.

Though they were allowed to live together on Quatcho land, Nakani's people had also shunned them. Fearful of starting a war with the Mazikeen, no one spoke to them. No one helped to build the traditional home. And when she became pregnant, no one offered to witness the birth. They were both barred from the Quatcho life tree.

It had been with sadness that Nakani and Fia headed out on their own, in search of a life tree that was apart from both Mazikeen and Quatcho. A tree that would welcome their child and bless it with the anamadraí—the soul magic—as it once existed before the great division of the forest people.

Fia let out a gasp as the pain rocked her once more. "Oooooooooo." She turned from Nakani's caress and reached high to the first oak branch, letting her weight hang from her hands, stretching her arms and sides, letting her abdomen stretch toward the tree. Mazikeen were not built to give birth. To keep the race pure, and to stop the pain of childbirth, Mazikeen babies could only be created from the magic borne of two Mazikeen lovers and they were born with the magic of a Mazikeen midwife who spirited the babe from the womb without pain.

She breathed deeply as the pain subsided. "How have your women survived so long giving birth without magic?"

"Time has taught them to bear it," Nakani said. "And they have grown stronger for it." He cuddled behind her and rubbed his hands on her belly, warming and soothing her. "I am sorry, Fia. I am sorry you must feel this. Your kind was not made for this type of birth."

"It is not your fault. It is mine." She panted through the next contraction and slumped against him. "This is my payment for deceiving you, for not telling you I wanted a baby."

"I would have done it anyway, had you asked." Nakani lifted her and placed her sitting with her back against the tree. He grasped her head and looked into her eyes. She could see only his love there—no anger, no hurt.

"Even knowing I would die, you would have agreed?"

Nakani lowered his eyes. His fingers trembled as they traced a pattern down her neck, across her shoulders and to the life tree itself. "I don't know. I believe I could have been convinced. I only wish we could find another way. Perhaps, if we had approached the dragons with a gift, they would have helped."

Fia pulled his face to her and kissed him long and hard. She wished she could ease his pain. She wished she could transfer her life force to see him through the trials she knew would come. But she could not. The only magic the Mazikeen could not take from her—her essence—would transfer to keep the child alive and safe. If Fia lived, the child would die. Their transgression had condemned themselves and the child at the moment of conception. There was no turning back now.

"What if..." Nakani's voice shook for a moment. He swallowed and her heart went out to him for his courage for staying with her, for still loving her and not making her take this final journey alone. "What if," he continued, "the babe is not strong?

What if she is not able to accept the anamadraí? What if the magic is too much for her? Then your death will be meaningless. I could not bear losing you for nothing, Fia."

Fia grasped his arms tight as a huge rush poured hot through her body and out her mouth. Ooooohhhhh-OOOOOHHHHHH. Straight-armed, she squeezed tight as the pain rolled through her. Once it subsided she leaned backed against the tree again as he continued to massage her bulging stomach. "We have been over this many times the last few months. Our only choice is to believe. We must act as though we believe. Please, Nakani, you must give me your promise."

Now the pains rolled over her so quickly she could no longer even cry out. Sweat poured from her petite frame straight into the soil. She looked up to the canopy of needled branches and focused on the honors others had left there. Fairy bells hung from branches fifty and a hundred feet from the ground. Decorations snaked around a rope secured to the trunk and woven across burls until reaching the leafed branches swaying high in the air above her. Dried, shriveled gourds clicked in the wind. Brightly colored scarves twisted and blazed a banner of life. The decorations of the past millennia marked each rebel birth and each death from those who dared to cross tribes—those who dared to love outside their kind.

"Here comes another...." Fia squatted with her hands in front of her like a cat on its haunches. "Soon," she mumbled. "The babe will be here soon."

Nakani placed himself on his knees in front of Fia, a towel slung over his wide shoulders. His massive frame blocked the light as he grabbed her hands and held them tight. Fia pressed her back against the Life Tree and she glowed like a candle in a crystalline lantern, her light obscuring all else around them. "You must promise," she said as another groan exited, followed by quick breaths. "This child will not be born without your promise."

"It is time to push," he said.

Soon Fia felt her skin bulging. "OohhOOOHHHH-Hooohhh," she cried as the babe's head crowned and another contraction moved the child swiftly down the canal. One more push, and a low cat-like growl worked its way up from her belly to her lungs and came out in a screeching yell. "Promise meeeeeeeeeeeee, now!"

Nakani took her face between his massive hands. Tears pooled on the fur below his eyes. "I promise," he finally said, his low voice fracturing with the words as they were ripped from him with each birth pang she endured.

"Thank you." Fia took his hands and placed them on the ground in front of her. "It is time." With one last push, the babe slipped right into his hands.

Nakani wrapped the child, quickly massaging away the light blue skin, checking for breath, toweling it to a natural blush. He smiled. "A girl, as you foretold." He put the babe in Fia's arms as she swayed against the tree and curled the baby toward her, offering her breast for the first and only Mazikeen milk the babe would get.

"Drink well." Fia coaxed the tiny mouth to suckle. "You must take all of it, and live." The babe pulled hungrily. "I give you the light of the Ahren Mazikeen," Fia intoned. "The power and strength of the Quatcho, and the eternal love of the forest."

Then, before his eyes the babe took on Fia's likeness and smiled up at him. Nakani smiled through tears. At least the child would have her mother's beautiful face. As long as the babe continued to drink, Fia would remain with him. She would not give up her life force until the girl was filled.

It seemed like only minutes, but perhaps it was an hour

when the child stopped and disengaged from Fia's breast, full and tired. Nakani watched helplessly as Fia weakened and the golden aura around her faded in and out.

"Here," Fia offered the child to him, her arms shaking with the effort. "Hold her while I prepare myself."

He pulled the babe to his chest and the child woke in his embrace. Her eyes opened wide and she giggled. Her body changed quickly, now showing fur from head to toe like any Quatcho babe.

They both sucked in a breath.

"A chameleon," Fia said. "It is the prophecy."

Settling her clothing around her, Fia gestured weakly for him to sit with her. He gently placed the child back in her arms —even though her arms now appeared to be insubstantial.

Fia kissed the fuzz of dark hair on the babe's head and the babe changed again to Mazikeen. "It will not be easy for you, little one," she said. "We have been waiting for you for five millennia." Fia's eyes closed then and her breathing began to labor. "You must… take her now… to Bliant. The trees will have sung her birth around the world. The People will know and they will come searching."

Nakani shook his head. "I will take her, but not yet. Not until …" He couldn't finish the sentence. His tongue refused to form the words his heart closed off.

"What shall we name her?" he asked, putting off the end as long as possible.

"Her forest name is Wynbune, but her Agnoses name shall be Camryn. She will need it on the other side," Fia whispered. "Tell Bliant her name is Camryn."

Wynbune now rested on the lichen as Fia's back and hips disappeared into the tree. Only the outlines of her legs and feet were visible in the lichen.

Nakani brushed his lips across hers once more, holding the sweetness of her kiss, pushing his breath into her to help her live one more minute.

"I have always loved you," she sighed out the words. "It is done. Please, stand to the side. I would see the light one last time."

He easily lifted the babe into one arm and stood to the side. Wynbune struggled and stretched her tiny hand toward her mother. His other hand clasped tight to Fia's arm as she raised it to the sky calling the sun's rays to end her life.

The dappled light streamed toward her, welcoming her back to be one with the forest. He watched her radiance until he could no longer distinguish any part of her body. He could see nothing except a pulsing glow against the life tree, spattered with the green lichen. Soon, a misty fog slid along the rays and he felt her arm and then her hand slip from him. The fog lifted and the light illuminated the bare ground with a new white trillium in Fia's stead.

Nakani kneeled on the lichen below the tree, rocking the babe as he wept.

Wynbune let out a keening cry, and an owl swooped over Wynbune's head and perched in the tree above them in broad daylight. Thunder Dragon song echoed through the forest. Wolves howled in the distance, and a lone unicorn pounded past them, its hooves stomping a wail as it disappeared in the fog. A low moan moved deep in the earth shaking the ground in sorrow.

THE END

*F*ifteen is too young to be alone.

And scared.

Camryn pulled the heavy curtain aside just enough to peer into the dark. The isolated log cabin sat on the edge of thousands of acres of redwood forest. With the moon obscured by clouds, she could barely see the trees nearest to the house. The early spring rain had not stopped for the past two weeks and she feared the stream would soon overflow its banks. She dropped the curtain and sagged to the floor, her back against the wall near the front door.

"Please. Please come back."

She dialed her mom's cellphone for what seemed like the hundredth time. After three rings, voicemail kicked in. "Hello. You've reached the Painter family. We can't come to the phone right now. Please leave a message."

"Mom? Dad? Where are you? Please come back. I promise I'll try harder not to be a freak. I'll do the dishes. I'll take out the garbage. Anything you want. Please come home. I'm scared. I love you. I really do."

She listened to the silence on the end of the recording, trying to think of something more to say. Something that would make a difference. "I love you," she repeated, her voice tired and filled with tears that had long stuck in her throat.

Finally, she hung up.

She pointed her cell phone toward the darkened living room, barely illuminating the chaos that had become her daily life—the moonrise afghan on the couch where she'd been sleeping, the empty bottles of diet vanilla coke, the wrappers and wrappers of fruit and nut bars. A bowl of half-eaten Cheetos, another bowl of unshelled peanuts. The closed windows trapped the moldy smells from the rain, and her unwashed clothes reeked of the sickening, sour sweat of fear.

The first night her parents were gone, she hadn't really worried. In fact, she'd reveled in her freedom. She played any music she wanted, danced around the living room and ate junk food instead of the healthy meals her parents insisted on fixing. The second night they didn't come home, she tried to be an adult about it. She'd called her mom's number. Said she was worried she hadn't heard from them, and asked them to call. She said she understood if they needed a break from her. Just let her know, so she could plan and not worry. That was it. Very mature. Very normal.

By the third night, she was in a full-scale panic. She'd been adopted at birth, but these were the only parents she knew. Was it possible her parents didn't know the freak would never be normal? In the past year, her inability to control the changes had become worse. Now that she was fifteen, maybe they'd given up on helping her. Maybe they didn't want her anymore.

On the fourth night, she sat by the door all night, praying

something hadn't happened to them, alternating crying with dry-eyed episodes of bargaining with God. She refused to leave the door, as if by sitting there she could will them to come home. But what if…No, she couldn't do it, couldn't even allow the thought to fully form. They'd come back. They had to.

It had been a week since Camryn's parents had gone to the store sixty miles away. Seven nights of wondering if all the evil things she said to her parents had finally driven them away. She'd called them monsters. She'd said she'd rather be dead than a freak. She'd screamed in pain with each change, first turning into her mother and then into her father.

It must be hard to know your daughter would never have friends, never date, never marry. Maybe they finally couldn't take it anymore. Maybe they'd send the cops to take her away to some institution where freaks were kept permanently out of the public eye.

She was letting her imagination get away from her. Her parents had always been patient and loving. Much more patient than Camryn had been lately. She didn't know what was wrong with her. It seemed that all she did was scream and yell and cry and make mountains out of molehills.

She fingered the phone once more. If she were normal she'd call the police, and report them missing. But she couldn't. She wasn't normal. She couldn't trust herself with anyone except her parents. The police would never understand. They wouldn't know how to deal with a freak who turned into them the minute they entered the room.

Grr-eow. That drawn out sound, halfway between a cat's meow and a purring growl, was back. Camryn turned on the porch light and peered through the peephole to see if it was the same animal that had visited her the last two nights.

A cat the size of an adult cougar paced on the porch. But this was no ordinary cougar. Instead of the usual yellowish-brown coat, with an off-white belly, this large cat had primarily silky, black and brown fur spotted with specks of gold. She would have said it was a black panther but they didn't exist in North America.

The cat sniffed the air and turned directly toward her.

Camryn froze.

Koška waits.

Camryn shook her head. What was that? It was like a ghostly voice in her head. But that was impossible. Who was Koška? She stared back at the cat. No. Impossible. Being alone was really getting to her imagination.

Koška waits.

The cat stretched, took two turns in a circle, and then settled onto the porch directly in front of the door, its head turned toward the drive.

Camryn backed away from the door. "What the hell?" She must really be losing it. She knew she was a freak, but she never thought she was insane. She paced in front of the door, wondering what she should do. There weren't any magic pills to make talking cats go away. Maybe she just needed sleep. She hadn't showered, hadn't slept in more than fits and starts for the past week.

Yes. That was it. She just needed more sleep.

She peeked out the window again and the cat stood, its ears canted forward, then sprang from the porch into the woods. Camryn heard wheels tearing up the pea gravel drive, spitting rocks behind them. The car sounded heavier than her parent's sedan, and it drove faster. Her parents never drove that fast up the drive.

She quickly turned off the porch light and slammed the deadbolt in place. She cowered next to the door.

"Drive past. Drive past. No one is home," she whispered.

The car stopped.

Heavy doors slammed closed. At least two sets of leaden footsteps crunched toward the front door.

Pound. Pound. A pause. *Pound. Pound.* The fisted knock echoed the pummels of her heart against her ribs. She held her breath.

"Miss Painter, it's the police. We're here to help. Open the door." A deep, weighty voice spoke.

Camryn squeezed her eyes closed. No! She wouldn't listen. *Don't talk. Don't talk. Please don't talk.*

She heard a slow outlet of breath near the door, as if whatever was to come next was burdensome. "We know you're alone. We just want to talk." A female voice, low, grave.

The doorknob jiggled but the deadbolt held. "Please, Miss Painter," the female coaxed. "Open the door."

Another heavy sigh.

"Camryn? " The deep voice was back. "It's about your parents."

Bile in her stomach rammed into her throat.

Fighting her will, the anchor on her chest pushed out the magma of sound. "Noooooooooo!" She sank to the floor, wrapped her arms around her stomach and rocked against the wall, hitting her back with each breath. "Go away! Go away! Go away!"

Boom! The front door splintered. *Boom! Boom!* The door exploded into the room.

Camryn screamed and ran.

Voices called. Lights blared. Faces appeared. Arms pulled.

A woman cop held Camryn tight against her bosom, suffocating the scream.

The cop stroked Camryn's head. "It's okay. Deep breaths now."

Camryn's breathing slowed and she raised her head to look at her captor. Camryn jerked as her vision blurred and sharp tingles on her scalp warned her of the coming change. Her hair grew longer as the shower of a thousand stings worked its way from her head to her chest. She grew taller, older. No. Stop. Stop!

She was becoming the cop.

She had to get away before they found out. Camryn kicked the cop in the shin and pushed.

"Crap!" The cop still held tight, but she listed to one side favoring the bruised leg.

Camryn squirmed and kicked again. Her fingernails reached to scratch any skin—face, arms, anything to get the cop to let go. She had to get away before they saw the freak.

"Why you little...stop it!" The cop shook her hard. "Calm down. We're not gonna hurt you."

Pain worked its way from her stomach to her toes like the ripple of sheet lightning. Her nerve endings fought against the change. Her skin stretched, her lips thickened, her hair grew toward her shoulders. She slammed her knee into the woman's stomach and then stomped on her instep.

Release! Camryn turned and ran blindly, her hands covering her face so they couldn't see what she had become.

The man grabbed her around the waist from the back and pinned her arms against her sides.

"Let me go! Let. Me. Go." She yanked and pulled to get away.

"Oh my god," the female yelled to her partner. "Look!" She pointed at Camryn. "She...she's...my twin."

The tall man turned her around. "What the hell?" He took her now thick, long, auburn hair in his fingers, stared at her face, her eyes. His gaze dropped lower, then snapped above her head. "That's impossible. No one can look exactly like you. Not in every detail."

Camryn felt the change start again as male whiskers sprouted on her chin. She looked away, bending around him, openly staring at the female cop. Focus. Focus on the woman. She cataloged every physical feature of the female cop, chanting the details to herself—shoulder length blonde hair, triangle face, bushy eyebrows, tight lips…. She held her breath as she focused, hoping that not breathing could prevent any further changes.

Finally secure in the image, she let out the breath and her shoulders sagged. "They're dead." Camryn was proud her voice shook only a little.

The policewoman nodded, her eyes still wide as she stared at Camryn. "Yes." The cop's speech strained, as if she had to force each word out. "Car accident. Down a steep cliff. Into the water." She finally looked away. "I'm sorry."

As each day had passed, Camryn suspected the truth—but she'd refused to put words to it. As if words alone had the strength to change reality. She'd rather believe her parents had abandoned her than to believe they had died. Now the cops were here to end all hope.

The female cop approached very slowly. "I can't believe how much you look like me. I never knew anyone could… I never…"

The man snapped his head in her direction stopping the cop's next words. Camryn kept her eyes on the woman. Maybe they'd treat her better because she looked like the female cop.

The man placed solid hands on Camryn's shoulders, making sure she didn't move. "We have a place for you to go," he said. His voice sounded caring, but she didn't trust him. "Someone to take care of you."

Camryn didn't look at him. Instead, she hung her head and kept the image of the policewoman in her mind. Please. Please don't change now. Please.

When she was a child, she used to be able to control what her body did when she was scared or nervous. The calming exercises her mother taught her used to work, and when they didn't she'd crawl into her mother's lap and they'd breathe… together. But not anymore. Not since sixth grade when she'd become the cursed, the demon, the freak. That's when her parents finally pulled her out of school—or rather the school forced her parents to teach her at home.

Now every time Camryn focused on someone, she turned into them. Man, woman, child, it didn't matter. She had little control over it and, since she'd reached puberty, the changes happened faster and became more painful every day.

Her parents insisted her changes were a gift—a gift she only needed to learn how to use. They'd said all teenagers had a hard time with their emotions. It's just that she was special, because her emotions caused her to become someone else. They promised it would pass. They'd lied.

"That's better," the policeman was saying. He must have taken her silence for acquiescence. "Now that you've calmed down a bit, we can talk. We can work out what's best for you. Okay?"

Camryn tensed under his hands. No way was talking going to change anything. Deep breaths. She needed to take deep breaths. Concentrate. Concentrate! She shifted her gaze back to the woman. Concentrate on the woman. Stay with her. Stay. With. Her.

"Let's all sit down for a moment," the man said, his voice almost a monotone now like he was trying to hypnotize her or something.

He urged her toward the middle of the sofa. The woman sat on one end.

"That's right," he said. "You're doing great. Let's all sit together right here. Okay?"

His hand on her shoulder pressed down and she perched on the edge, ready to run at the first chance she could find.

He slowly removed his hands and sat on the other side. He turned toward her, his shin and knee at a forty-five degree angle to her leg, effectively trapping any sudden movement she might make. He looked casual but Camryn knew better. She'd seen this ploy before with the Principal before she was kicked out of school. She scooted a few inches away.

The cop leaned forward to close the space. "I know this is hard for you. Let's take a few minutes and talk. That's all. Just talk."

She looked up at him and swallowed as she tried to form a smile that would make her appear normal, maybe even thankful. She could do this. She could be calm. She could be... nonfreak if she concentrated.

He smiled back and she liked his smile. He wasn't all that old. Not as old as her parents. In fact, she'd guess he was maybe twenty-five or so. Way too old for her, but he seemed nice. Maybe he wouldn't be like the others. Maybe he would understand.

Pain. Thousands of small razors sawed their way down her arms. Her vision blurred again and she cried out in pain. No. No. No. Not now. But it wouldn't stop. It never stopped.

She jumped up and he grabbed her arm. "Now, now," he said. "You were doing so well. Come on, sit back down. Everything's fine. No need to be scared."

She never should have looked at him. She never should have smiled. The change came faster than before. Her face broadened to match his. Her chin sprouted facial hair. Her hair turned blonde and shortened to the same crew cut the policeman sported.

The woman cop screamed and backed off.

Camryn had to look away. She had to find a different focus. She turned toward the woman cop but she couldn't focus as the man forcefully turned her back toward him.

"Holy mother of..." The cop dropped his grip on her arm and she sprinted toward the kitchen, kicking over the large popcorn can. She raced around the portable kitchen island, then shoved it hard toward the living room. She heard him swear as the island hit him.

"She's running," he shouted to his partner as his boots crunched across the popcorned carpet. "Get around back."

Camryn pushed through the back door, jumped from the porch over two concrete steps, slid in a muddy patch, and then regained her balance and raced into the woods behind the house. Thunder boomed, echoing the roar in her head as the clouds opened up. Rain, hard and unforgiving, drove daggers into her arms.

Stupid. Stupid. Stupid. What ever made her think she could hold herself together? Didn't she ever learn? No one knew how to deal with the freak. No one.

Camryn knew these woods. She could lose the cops in the forest. She'd stay for however long she needed. She'd been camping. She could survive. Couldn't she? It didn't matter anyway. Her parents were dead. No one would ever understand her again. She loved the woods. If anything in the fairy tales were true, the woods would protect her.

She'd leave it to nature to decide her fate. She was supposed to be with her parents. She was supposed to die. It was up to the forest now.

The cops shouted and boots pounded on the path behind her. Camryn veered cross-country and struggled uphill. Redwoods towered around her. Nothing she could climb. The voices grew closer. She needed to get deeper into the forest where she could hide. She swung around a tree and headed further uphill, away from the path. With every step, her body changed again. Each change painful. Each change slowing her. She had no idea what she looked like now, who her body had chosen to become.

Lungs burning, desperate for air, forced her to slow her pace. When her legs refused to climb any more, Camryn came to rest against a charred giant redwood. She circled the tree and found what she wanted, a small hole carved out of the bottom by a long ago fire. The scar was on the back side, the side facing uphill and not easily noticed. She'd be safe. Please, God, she prayed. Let me be safe, just for a while. Just for once.

Cold and gasping for air, she stepped out of the rain and crawled into the wounded embrace of the scorched tree. Rich, earthy decay assaulted her senses. Camryn's rain-soaked t-shirt spread a chill through her now petite child-framed bones. Her shoulder-length, chestnut hair had returned, clinging to her cheeks in muddy streaks. She shivered in the safety of the hollowed out trunk, and the wind howled angrily back at her as if disappointed that she had escaped the storm.

Dead. No matter how far she ran, it did not change the situation. Her parents were dead. Dead before she learned how to stop the curse. Dead before she learned how to control her changes. Dead before she was ready for...anything. She pounded her fist against the trunk.

Camryn squeezed her eyes closed. The tears leaked beneath her lashes as she worked hard to gather her memories about her like a warm blanket. Finally, her breathing slowed. She could see everything so clearly now. The sun-bleached meadow that led to the house, the shadows the redwoods cast over the backyard, the creek that scraped a path between trees and sky. Those things were a part of her. They were all she had left. A part she would hold close, no matter what happened.

She had thought her home was nothing more than the barrier that kept her from freedom. But the truth was that her parents' love had kept much of the world's wickedness out. That love had sheltered her from the horror and panic of peers, the condemnation of preachers, the intolerance of her school-teachers. Her parents had accepted Camryn as she was, never asking her to be someone different. More than that, her parents believed Camryn had a unique gift, a special purpose. Without them, how would she ever learn what that purpose was?

Her teeth chattering, she shook with cold for what felt like hours. She curled into a ball on the forest duff inside the hollowed tree. Her breathing and heart rate slowed as drowsiness claimed her. Her eyes closed and she gave herself up to the cold. She had only to remain silent a little longer and the decision would be made.

Camryn, No! A woman's voice screamed inside Camryn's head. Get up! Get up! But Camryn couldn't open her eyes, couldn't move. Instead, she curled tighter and burrowed into the pine needles and dead leaves until only her head poked out for air. A kaleidoscope of dreams kept her from any peace she might find in oblivion —the forest burning, faeries churning, monsters stirring.

The feel of a warm tongue lapped against her face. *Koška ... Koška wakes... Koška wakes.* Camryn fought through the fog of dreams. A large cat with spotted fur and tufted ears lay curled against her. Camryn rose slowly to a sitting position, squeezing her eyes shut and then opened them again, testing whether she was still dreaming. The cat stilled, sat and stared for a moment. It looked familiar, like the one on her porch over the past three days. Still unsure of reality, she reached toward it, like a pet, and the cat skittered out of the tree, the white spot on its short bobbed tail highlighting a trail in the dark.

Camryn blinked and shook her head of dreams. Was the cat called Koška? Had the cat spoken? No. That was impossible. Maybe she was going crazy. Maybe she really needed help. Camryn stood, working out the kinks of muscles held too tight. The memory of the woman's voice still echoed in her mind. The voice seemed familiar, and caring, but she couldn't place it. It wasn't her mother's voice. She shook her head. It was probably another hallucination, just like the large cat.

Dying wasn't the answer. Her parents were no longer here to shelter her from the world...from the normals. But they would want her to live. They would want her to find her purpose. She would have to find a way to live in the real world. She would have to find a way to control the changes.

Staying apart from the world wasn't the answer. Her parents had meant well, but she was done being sheltered. She needed help and her only choice was to trust the cops. They were supposed to help homeless children find a home, weren't they? Maybe they could find a therapist too—someone who could teach her to control the changes.

Stepping out of the tree's embrace, Camryn listened for voices. First she heard dogs, then she heard men. She walked toward the cops' voices praying she could, for once, keep herself together. She bargained again with God. Just this once, could I not go through the change? Just this once, please help me to hold it together until I find a new home.

THE PROPHECY

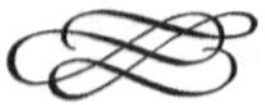

scourge born of the Agnoses shall permeate the forest network and cause great suffering among the People. Taking no heed of gender or class, of good or evil deeds, it will magnify the power of the dark and extinguish light for all tribes.

The Queens of the Mazikeen and the Quatcho, the Spirits of the Cloud Forests and the Great Bear, the Boha'a wanderers and the Mau shall plead to the void to end their suffering.

Behold, at the dawn of the fifth millennia of the People, a half-breed child shall be born. Her name will be called Wynbune, the Chameleon. She shall be gifted as the strongest mage of all time. She alone can wield the powers of light and darkness with the blessing of the void. She alone can control not only the forest network, but the life-giving force of the void itself.

Therefore, all those who dwell in the forest must nurture the child and her parents, so that she grows in wisdom and understanding. Choose wisely the healer who will prepare the Chameleon for the Kintala, when the powers of the void are fully imbued.

Beware! If the powers of the dark dominate the Kintala, the Chameleon will destroy all of the People in her attempt to survive. Only the Agnoses, deaf to the use of magic to control the light and dark, will survive.

Be Assured! If the powers of light dominate the Kintala, the Chameleon will destroy the scourge of the Agnoses, and the People will thrive once more.

Blessed be understanding. Blessed be the Void. Blessed be the People.

~

OHAR MOVED QUICKLY up the winding path toward the mother tree. He had been summoned and, if what he'd heard from his thunder dragon was true, his life was no longer his own.

"Ohar, wait."

It would be easier to run from Lyra as she ran to catch up, but he couldn't do it. It wouldn't be fair to leave her without an explanation.

Her waist-length golden hair flew behind her, streaming sunshine in its wake. She carried so much light inside her that he hated to be the one to bring this darkness to her life. He wasn't ready to say goodbye.

"What's happened?" Lyra asked, her hands reaching to frame

his face. "Why are you rushing? Is the queen finally ready to bless our marriage?"

Ohar took a deep breath and shook his head. "It is the prophecy. The Chameleon has been found. You know what that means."

Her eyes expressed every emotion he also felt. Denial. Anger. Grief. Confusion. Even her sunshine hair dulled as her eyes filled with tears.

"No! It can't be," she whispered. "She was lost to us. Even the queen thought she was lost to us."

"Koška has found her, and when I tell my mother the news I know what she will say."

"Then don't tell her," Lyra begged. "Don't tell her until we determine what else can be done. I can't lose you. Not now."

"You know my mother has the sight. She probably already knows. If I don't tell her, it will seem that I am disloyal, that I don't want to save the Mazikeen."

Lyra shook her head forcefully. "But, how do you know for sure? Perhaps Koška is mistaken. Perhaps—"

Ohar silenced her with a kiss. Pulling her closer, he lingered on her mouth, pouring his final goodbyes into the kiss. He'd hoped his mother was mistaken when she said the Chameleon lived among the Agnoses. He'd even hoped that Lyra could be the one to fulfill the prophecy, and his mother just couldn't see it. Her visions of the future were always cloudy—never exact. But now he knew for sure it wasn't Lyra. It never would be.

He lifted his head and hugged her tight. "I'm sorry. I should not have pursued you. I knew this day would come. My mother had foretold it from the time we began courting. I just didn't want to believe."

Lyra's tears soaked his shirt now. "Three years," she said,

choking out the words between her sobs. "I thought ... I hoped..."

"The queen is never wrong." Ohar ground out the statement between clenched teeth, and gently pushed Lyra from him. "Please, do not follow me, do not seek me out. Mother will kill you if she believes you are a threat to her plan."

Lyra took a step back, her head lowered, eyes on the ground. Then another. Then another.

"You must open yourself to someone else. You can find love again, Lyra. You can."

"No. I can't," she said, her fists clenching at her side as she lifted her gaze back to him. "I refuse."

"I know it is hard now, but you have too much love in you to not offer it to someone else. The Mazikeen need more people like you. We need mothers and wives like you. Please, Lyra. Please take your time to grieve but then you must move on, as I must."

"If I cannot love you, I will love no one. " She backed away further.

He stepped to her and held her close again. "No. Don't say that. I can't do what I must if I believe you are alone. Promise me you will consider someone else. Please, Lyra."

She extended her neck and her arms to the clear skies above and called out in a tear-strained voice. "Karith."

Storm clouds roiled overhead and thunder sounded. Ohar looked up, recognizing Lyra's thunder dragon as she spiraled toward them. The green, iridescent wings flashed as lightning illuminated her descent. Karith landed softly and offered a leg for Lyra to easily hoist to her back. Lyra stretched forward, wrapping her hands in riding straps.

"I will always love you, Ohar. I will always seek you out." Then she turned her face away from him. "Therefore, I must make sure I cannot find you. I must make sure I do not interfere." Saying nothing more, the dragon and Lyra immediately disappeared.

"Nooooooooooo!" Ohar yelled to the sky, his arms raised in protest. "Not the zwichen. Not the void."

HOURS LATER, Ohar trudged up the final hill to the mother tree. He had refused to use the forest network to hurry to his mother. A few hours would make no difference in his duty. He had needed the time to grieve Lyra before facing his mother. Exhausted, he entered into the queen's realm and straightened to his full height. No matter his pain, he must turn his attention to his duty. He would not allow the Mazikeen to die because of his loss.

The twenty-two elders wore their traditional council garments: a white cotton tunic, tied around the waist with a leather belt. Over the tunic was a scapula, a garment consisting of a long, wide piece of grey cloth worn over the shoulders with an opening for the head. The scapular was secured with a pewter circle pin inscribed with sacred runes. Inside the circle were pewter leaves representing the sacred Oak, Holly, and Ivy. Oak is Nature's magician and representative of the gateway trees in all forests. Holly guards against evil spirits, and Ivy stands for fidelity of the council with the Forest People.

Ohar's mother, Queen Mayja, emerged from the split trunk of the Oak gateway tree before him. The bark melded with the lower half of her body, while from the waist up she appeared mostly human like the ancestors of all forest Mazikeen. Though she had been this way since Ohar was a toddler, he still wished she could separate from the tree and walk with him, offer a hug or a touch. He wished she could be as other mothers among the People—someone who cared what he wanted, how he felt, someone who could take a moment to understand his heartbreak and offer solace.

He shook his head. She hadn't touched him since he was nine. At seventeen it was unlikely she ever would again. She said her attention was focused on keeping the Mazikeen pure and stopping the mutations which caused children to burn bright and die before they had a chance to undertake the Kintala.

Ohar's sisters believed their mother's choice to become a permanent part of the forest network meant she was highly infected by the lichen mutations. They pointed to her sudden bursts of anger, followed by quiet understanding only moments later. They believed she was drunk on power and could no longer be trusted to keep the Mazikeen safe.

"Your hair is colorful today," Ohar said, putting off the news he had to share. A combination of lichen and leaves wreathed through her multicolored hair. Strands of red and brown and blonde rioted with pink and blue, grey and white, as if she couldn't make up her mind what color she wanted it to be.

"We have felt a change," Queen Mayja said, her voice rising to a screech on the last word. "The singing trees are no longer able to keep out the Agnoses." She spit out her disgust with the humans beyond the magic barrier. "The scryers have looked into the pool and seen the mixed-blood child alive in the Agnoses world. The one named Wynbune—who was brought into this world against my command." The entire tree rained leaves upon them as his mother shook when she said the name. "The child the Quatcho hid and refused to bring to us."

Ohar wondered if Nakani was still imprisoned by his mother. Ohar only knew the Quatcho's name because he had heard rumors as a child of a hairy one who dared to go against the Queen and was banished to the ice caves. Whenever Ohar thought of rebelling against his mother's edicts—particularly when it came to her proclamations on his love life—the story of Nakani had always stopped him.

"She will turn sixteen in a fortnight," the Queen continued. "The Kintala has already risen in her. If she is not brought to the forest and put under our control soon, her power will be unleashed by the Agnoses and we will all perish."

A murmur of agreement passed from one elder to the next.

"All Mazikeen?" Ohar asked, knowing his mother was not beyond exaggeration for effect. "Even those of the other forests?"

"Yes," the Queen whispered and closed her eyes. "All." She shimmered and melded with the tree as if it was too much for her to bear. The council gasped in response.

Ohar watched her carefully, refusing to react to this bit of manipulation. He knew that sometimes she performed a little drama to get others to do things that may be distasteful. He wondered what her plan was this time.

After a few moments, she seemed to regain herself and returned to reveal her full upper body again. His mother gestured for him to rise. "There has never before been one so powerful. Ohar, you are the one I choose to stop her destruction of the Mazikeen."

Ohar had lived long enough to know that the politics of power among the Mazikeen was fought in a game of semi-truths, a game that often exaggerated potential peril in order for someone to gain power or to get others to do things they would not normally do.

He bowed again to his mother and touched his chest. "How can only one man hold back such power? Surely, my Queen should send an army of warriors to face down this child if she is so dangerous."

The Queen sighed loudly and then pointed at him. "He questions my wisdom even now. My own son doubts my word."

He rose in denial. "Mother, I do not. I did not say…"

"Silence," she yelled, her face beet red and her teeth clenched so tight he wondered if the skin on her face might break off in sheets and expose the skeleton beneath. "Do not deny your language tricks. I know them all. You pretend innocence when you are not. You pretend weakness when you are not. You take my affection for you as permission to try me. I do not give you permission."

He went back to one knee and bowed his head. It would not help his cause to make her angry. "I ask forgiveness. You are right, I overstepped. I should have accepted my queen's command without question."

"Yes, yes." She let out another loud breath for all to hear. "You are forgiven as always." She gestured toward the council, a smug smile on her lips. "What is a mother to do but forgive her only son?"

An uneasy titter, laughter laced with fear, made its way through the council members.

His mother drew herself up and gestured for Ohar to rise again.

He stood, his spine straight and looked his mother in the eye.

"Now attend to my words," she spoke in measured meter as if he was too slow to understand. "I will only speak them once. I do not stretch the truth here. You are the only one I can trust on this mission. My daughters connive to take my place as Queen and would use this event to their advantage, not to the advantage of the Mazikeen."

Ohar nodded. His sisters were much more rebellious than he.

"But they will not succeed!" The Queen promised. "Gather close my council and learn what I have seen in the void."

The twenty-two council members moved with Ohar to stand in a tight knot, each touching some part of the gateway tree from which the queen emerged.

"I call the power of the void," she intoned.

Her arms reached toward the sky and the wind whipped above the trees. She circled her hands above her head and the air crackled with power. "Behold the vortex of understanding." The sound of air rushing around them was almost deafening. The change in pressure pressed Ohar and the council down, as if a weight were upon them. The trees shook until their needles fell into the swirling wind. Then they gathered and spun in the air like a tornado gathering power. They sat in the eye of the storm, with the wind and the needles spinning so fast that no one could pass into or out of the magic circle.

"Silence!" the Queen commanded. Though the power of the vortex remained just as strong, the roar of the wind no longer assaulted them.

"The presence of the Chameleon has been told to me by my best source among the Agnoses," his mother continued." Sela has personally witnessed the Chameleon's powers and has reported that they are stronger than any Mazikeen she has witnessed. She also reports that the Agnoses drugs have intensified the Chameleon's power and courted the dark side. This when she is only four years past menses."

"If the Agnoses have entrapped her," the leader of the elders said. "Then she will die or burn out like the other Mazikeen. Perhaps we should let that happen. Not mount a rescue."

"No!" The queen shook her head side to side so violently

that the trunk of the tree split in two and, for a moment, it appeared as if two queens faced them. After a pause, the two queens melded into one again and the split on the right worked the bark further up the queen's chest to secure her once more within the gateway tree. "Do you not remember the rest of the prophecy? Do you not remember that if the Chameleon chooses the light she will save the Forest People and finally destroy the Agnoses?"

The council members mumbled in confusion.

"You don't want her killed then?" Ohar asked, swallowing his fear. He was not sure he could kill even if commanded by the queen.

"I am not as cruel as you think, Ohar. Killing is only of the last resort," she said. "I want to save her…to help her. But she must choose to be helped and that is where you will be of assistance."

"So, I am to kidnap her then and bring her to you."

"No. She must come of her own will or she could unleash her anger and destroy us. You must befriend her, offer your protection, get her to trust you, to follow you.

"What am I to tell her that would induce her to follow me?"

"This is why you are the only one to go, Ohar. This is where your skills in language can finally be used for good, instead of annoying me. It is up to you how much to share. Say whatever you must to get her here…but share as little as possible."

Ohar smiled. "That sounds easy enough."

"It is not easy," the Queen snapped. "Your soul will be in grave danger every moment you are with her. You will be naturally attracted to her, maybe even believe you are in love with her, but it is not real and you must deny its pull. It is only her siren song."

Ohar flinched. He did not want to fall in love with anyone ever again. His love was for Lyra, even if she was gone forever.

He forced a laugh from his throat. "I have dealt with sirens before. It can be fun."

"You are not to dally with her, Ohar, as she doesn't know the power of her own song and in the throes of passion she could unleash her powers and…"

"Destroy us," Ohar finished for her. "I understand."

"Do not take this lightly," she warned. "I can hear in your voice that you don't believe everything I say. I am deadly serious, Ohar. All of Mazikeen is at risk. This is not a trick. This is the truth."

He looked at her and they locked gazes. He searched her eyes but they were blank to him. He had learned how to read her aura over the years, but sometimes she didn't even allow an aura to reveal at all. This was one of those times. He knew that she believed her words. But he wasn't sure if it was truth. After what seemed like several minutes of them standing face to face, unflinching, he dropped his gaze.

He finally capitulated and said what she would expect. "I see you tell the truth. How do I find her?"

Queen Mayja flicked her fingers and the vortex stopped swirling. "Leave us know," she said to the rest of the council. "What I say now is for my son's ears only." She waited until the others had left then closed her eyes.

Ohar immediately felt her push on his mind.

"She is in a place the Agnoses call Starlight Center." He heard her voice in his mind. He understood this would keep their conversation completely private.

"You must convince her to leave quickly," his mother said. "Her body is ready for the Kintala. She must be brought to me to prepare to survive the tests." She paused. "Then on her seventeenth birthday you will wed, and by her eighteenth birthday she will bear her first Mazikeen child."

"All this you have seen in your visions?"

"Yes!" She sent a vision of complete confidence, then frowned and shook her head. "Of course, my visions are not exact. But I know this is what needs to happen. I know this is the way to save the Mazikeen. It is your combined DNA that will provide a way to stop the lichen mutations."

Ohar worried the inside of his cheek. He knew the prophecy as well as any Mazikeen child, but it was short on details. He'd never understood how fathering children with a half Mazikeen, half Quatcho woman would change anything. He also knew his mother. She didn't always tell him the whole truth. He was sure there was something more to her plan.

"Are you sure this is the right path?" he asked. "I do not understand how this changes anything. How I could not simply marry a pure Mazikeen and do the same thing."

She flicked her wrist and rain poured all around them, drenching him but leaving her dry. Now she spoke in normal conversation. "Here, the forest cries for you and that silly Lyra. Are you satisfied now?" Just as quickly the rain stopped.

Ohar balled his hand into a fist, wishing he could let his temper reign, but he would not give her the satisfaction of seeing him explode. "As if you even cared about Lyra or me."

"Tsk, tsk, temper is so unattractive in a prince, don't you think? You were raised better than that."

"Yes, I was, no thanks to you."

Queen Mayja laughed, shooting little flames from her mouth and burning the understory around the tree. He ached as each bush sizzled and died.

"You don't have to kill things to show your power," he said.

"And you don't have to love me," she countered. "You don't

even have to like me. But you will obey me." The ground shook with her command. "You will obey me because you want to save our people just as much as I do."

Ohar said nothing for several minutes. He wished he could find another way, someone else to take on this task, but he knew his mother would never let that happen. Somehow, she was sure that Ohar and Wynbune's paths were intertwined in the prophecy and without him it would not come true.

He let go of his anger and squared his shoulders as he faced her. "Tell me where to find her."

His mother put a picture in his mind. The route would take him across the Mazikeen protected lands and into the Agnoses interface in the forest. He would follow the river to the sea after crossing the Singing Trees. Then he would travel south along the bluff to Mayu where he would find a square building surrounded by redwood forest. The building was similar to many others where Mazikeen had been taken and tortured, often never to return.

"Is she hurt?" he asked, well aware of the tales told by the few Mazikeen who had escaped similar Agnoses torture chambers.

"They are forcing her to use her powers. But she is not cowed yet. But she will die if you don't convince her to come with you. If she dies, all of us die."

"And if she refuses to marry me?"

"Then you must use all of your power to convince her. There are ways."

"I will not use my powers to hurt her, to threaten her."

"Then threaten the Agnoses. Even without family, surely she would fear us killing her kind."

"That is not our way. That is not the way of the Mazikeen, the way of the light."

The queen laughed again, this time ice crackled along the bark that held her and froze the ground between them. "There will be no Mazikeen way if she doesn't accept. Don't you understand that? We will all die. All of us! Is that what you want?"

Ohar didn't say anything back, but he vowed he would not cross that line, not if there was any way to avoid it. He didn't know Wynbune at all. Maybe she would come without question. But he did know his mother, and he didn't trust her. Since letting the darkness in, power had corrupted her. He knew there was more to her plan that she let on.

As quickly as the ice had formed, the sunshine returned and melted the ice away. His mother softened her voice. "There are other ways besides killing. You can tell her about her father. We still have him imprisoned. You could offer his freedom in exchange for her agreement to marry."

"I will not bargain like that. That is not the way to take a wife and have her content."

The queen sighed loudly. "Fine. Then seduce her in the same ways you enjoyed with Lyra." She put a picture in his mind of him making love with Lyra in the forest, her golden hair spread across his nude body.

He turned from her and blocked the picture from his mind. "We did not get that far and you know it. I would not seduce simply for my own pleasure. We were waiting until after marriage. If you indeed have the sight you know Lyra and I…" He could not finish the sentence. He turned back and shook a finger at her. "Don't ever put a picture of Lyra in my mind again. If you do, I will walk away forever."

His mother laughed again, this time so hard the ground shook. "How did I raise someone who at seventeen has still not seduced a girl? You should be ashamed."

Ohar turned his back and began walking.

"Ohar," she called. "I apologize. It was cruel."

He stopped. It would be so easy to leave, so much easier than doing what she asked. Finally he turned back to her, but he stood in place, not willing to get closer again.

The queen quieted for a moment. "Love is not a requirement for marriage. The forest knows I did not love your father. It is not a requirement for you to love Wynbune. If she requires words of love to marry, then tell her a few lies. She's lived among the Agnoses, she will believe you."

"I will not lie," he said between clenched teeth.

"What will you do then?" she asked in a restrained voice. "What will you sacrifice to save your own people?"

Again, she put pictures into his mind. This time it was not a seduction but something more aggressive. He pushed back at her. It was the mutation. He had to believe that. The Mazikeen were not a violent people. They were more light than dark. They would not intentionally hurt anyone, even Agnoses.

In silence they fought. Ohar shutting his mind to her and the queen fighting to reopen it. He battled back, sending light into her darkness. He reached to the void for more power and the earth cracked between them, separating him from the mother tree.

Finally she released him with a sigh. "If the choice is that or her death, our death, which will you pick?"

"Neither," he said just as quiet, and with the full force of conviction. "I choose neither. The universe does not provide only two choices. It provides many. I will find another way. My way."

He turned his back again, this time swiftly moving into the forest, putting as much space between him and the mother tree as possible.

~

AFTER TWO DAYS of walking without rest, he found himself at the mouth of the Klamath River. He stared at the waves as they rolled to the sand. How long had it been since his mother had shifted more toward darkness than light? Why did he not notice? How many other Mazikeen were like her now?

Even the pounding of the surf did not offer him solace. He looked to the skies for Woytan. He needed to prepare.

He needed to find the will—the heart—to bring the Chameleon back to the forest. He needed to find a way to help her survive the Kintala without his mother getting to her first. He wished Lyra were still here. He could have trusted her to help Wynbune. Her soul was so filled with light, surely she would have been a good guide.

Ohar swallowed hard to stop tears from falling. Perhaps not. Perhaps it would have been too much to ask of Lyra. Could she have helped the one designated to be his wife? If the roles were reversed, he is sure he could not do it. Duty or not.

He would have to find another Mazikeen woman to guide Wynbune. Someone who wasn't afraid of the queen. Someone who understood the need to keep Wynbune safe for all the People, not just the Mazikeen.

He sent a silent call to Woytan. Lightning and thunder spread across the inlet and white clouds separated to usher in his bonded dragon. Soon he could differentiate the pure white scales and feathers emerging from the clouds. Woytan sailed over the ocean, trailing snow behind him until he settled in front of Ohar.

Woytan bowed low. *You are in need of meditation.*

Ohar nodded. *I need time in the zwischen.* He climbed aboard Woytan's back and pulled the straps around him.

You cannot seek Lyra and Karith.

Bending forward, Ohar wrapped an arm around the neck of his dragon. *I know. I need the gift of nothing.*

Time. Woytan said. *I will buy you time.*

Gently, the dragon lifted into the air. With each downbeat of his wings they climbed higher into the clouds. When they broke through, Ohar could see nothing of the ground.

The light, Woytan said. *Drink it in and prepare for the zwischen.*

Ohar gloried in the warm colors of the setting sun. He closed his eyes and pulled the rays toward him, drinking in as much light as his soul could contain.

His soul filled, he opened his eyes in the void.

SWEET SIXTEEN

Redwood Forests. Cats circling.
Cars crashing. Mother screaming.
Blood everywhere.
Darkness. Caskets. Arms carrying.
A needle injected.
Objects flying. Fire from her fingers.
Death. Destruction.
A needle injected.
Sleep. Awake. More drugs.
Sleep. Awake.

Camryn shivered in the pool of sweat clinging between the sheet and her body. It took her a second to realize that she'd clawed the top sheet away. Lying facedown on the threadbare bottom sheet, the heavy smell of bleach mixed with the saltiness of her fear. Her pillow lay on the floor, its pillowcase hung from the lamp beside her bed.

She groaned. Nightmares. Again.

Her dreamcatcher, one of the few things she'd been allowed to bring from her parents' home, still hung above her bed. For all the good it did.

When Camryn's parents were alive, her mother told her it would catch all the good dreams and save them in case she needed them again. Another lie. Now she wished it would catch her nightmares and never let them go. It didn't. In fact, the dreamcatcher didn't seem to work at all without her mother.

Slow down. Deep breath. Don't go there this morning. She wanted no sedatives on her birthday. That would really ruin everything. She sucked in air and counted to ten, then let it out slowly. Better.

She closed her eyes again and listened. Silence. Not shift change yet.

Every day at 6:45 the nurses changed shifts. Their whispered voices, as they shared greetings and information on the patients, was Camryn's natural alarm. Then precisely at 7:00 the institutional bell sounded, calling the insane out of their beds to face a new morning, to pretend for one more day that they could learn to be normal.

Normal. How could you be normal when no one wanted to touch you, when even the doctors made you sit away from them while asking those stupid questions that no girl in her right mind could answer. She smiled at her own joke and stretched. She couldn't answer them in her wrong mind either.

"Do you think you're crazy?" Dr. Frenelli always asked.

"I didn't used to, now I'm not sure."

"Do you ever talk to yourself?"

"Sure. There's no one else to talk to. I'd go insane if I didn't talk." She giggles.

"Do people tend to stare at you?"

"Duh! That's why I'm here, right? People don't like that I

look like them. I don't like it either, but there it is. Nothing I do seems to stop it."

"Are you worried about this test?"

And that's how it always went. Different questions, same results. Sometimes she wasn't sure who was more crazy—the doctors or her.

Forget about being crazy, she admonished herself. Today, be strong. She swung her legs over the edge of the bed and stood. Stomping to her closet like a soldier on a mission, Camryn kept her shoulders back, her straight arms swinging in step, her chin high. She yanked the pin out of the hasp. It dangled on a short, but strong clear wire. Throwing the door to one side she reveled in the loud bang. She was being silly. But who cared? Today she gave herself permission to act however she wanted.

In the faint light from the window, Camryn eyed the few pieces of clothing hanging from pegs in the open closet—no belts, no ropes, nothing that she could hurt herself with. She scanned her three white blouses. Next to them were three black pairs of pants, all exactly the same. Today was not a day to be boring. Today was a day to stand out. To stand tall. To be noticed instead of hiding in a corner trying to disappear. Today was her sixteenth birthday and she was going to celebrate.

Camryn reached to the top shelf and extracted a cardboard shoebox. She smiled at the hot pink, silk scarf carefully folded inside. They'd allowed her to keep it along with a few other scarves because it was so soft and flimsy it couldn't be used to hang herself. As if she was suicidal. If she'd wanted to die, she would have stayed in the forest instead of giving herself up to the police.

She fingered the scarf again, enjoying the feel of it. She'd bought this on her fourteenth birthday, determined to wear shocking colors to see if it would shock her body into revealing her one and only true self. It hadn't worked, but it still made her smile. She'd find a way to wear it today.

She pulled out her Pazito ballet flats from the far end of the closet. The light pink, floral print on a maroon background had a quilted patent toe. She hadn't worn these since she'd arrived at Starlight Center a year ago. She usually slummed it with sweats and slippers, but today was special and these shoes were just the ticket to carry off the hot pink accent of her scarf belt.

"Sixteen!" Camryn shouted, the word laced with unfettered hope. She'd been waiting for this magical sixteenth birthday to find out if "special" meant she was tagged for something great or if she was doomed to be alone. Her mother had promised her when she turned sixteen Camryn would finally understand who she is, why she was the freak. Her mother had promised to introduce her to someone who would help her with the changes—someone who could teach her how to control them forever.

She tucked in the long-sleeved white blouse and then pulled the hot pink, silk scarf through the belt loops of her pants, braiding it together in front to make a fashionable loop. Slipping on the shoes made her smile.

What will Dr. Frenelli say now? He'd be surprised by her outfit. He was all for rules and consistency, tradition and conformity. Today she didn't care what he thought. Today she would rebel.

Taking a deep breath, she closed her eyes, slowly rolled her shoulders twice, and let out the air. She wished for the millionth time that the high window in her room was lower, where she could see out to the redwood forest that surrounded Starlight Center. Then she could pretend she was in her room back home, a room with a picture window, a room with her mother sharing the view and telling fairy tales about the forest people—stories Camryn now craved.

She squeezed her eyes shut again, trying to bring back the feeling of her mother's touch. Her adoptive mother had been the only person who had dared to touch her every day once the changes started. Even her adoptive father shuddered a bit, knowing she would look like him if he gave her more than a moment of attention. It was no wonder her biological father had given her up so soon after birth. He must have known and couldn't deal with it. Both her adoptive parents had been wonderful about talking with her, listening to her, teaching her. But the thing she missed the most was not their faces nor their voices. It was their touch, the touch that told her she was still human, still lovable.

Camryn steeled herself to step in front of the small oval mirror across from her bed. It wasn't made of glass. That was deemed too dangerous. Instead it was a shiny, unbreakable plastic. At least it was better than no mirror at all.

Opening her eyes, she looked into the mirror. She saw her adopted mother looking back and she sighed. She kissed the fingers on her hand and touched the image in the mirror. Miss you. Her shoulders slumped. It was hard…so hard.

Camryn ran her fingers across her brows, then beneath her eyes from the bridge of her nose to her cheekbones, smoothing the age lines of the face staring back at her. The pain of the change was barely perceptible now. Over the past year at Starlight Center, she'd learned to control the stings and lightning along her skin. She'd practiced in secret—practiced changing more slowly. She wasn't always perfect, if she was in a crowd, or scared. But sometimes she could handle it and surprise herself.

She fingered the curls of her mother's short chestnut hair.

She searched her memory for a younger face. Camryn had no memory of what she'd looked like before the changes began. It was like every change wiped away a little more of her identity until she had none of herself left.

Instead, Camryn searched her memory for some other young girl, someone near her age she had met since coming to the Center. Yes. Carla. The girl's hair was a similar color but it was long and straight. She concentrated on the girl's hairstyle until her own hair lengthened almost to her waist. Then she added back some wave, almost a curl. Her mother always had a natural curl. She wanted to keep the nut-brown color of her mother's skin after a long summer, and she definitely wanted the pale blue eyes that had looked into hers with love every day of her memory.

She smiled at the mirror. Yes, this was a good image for today. Young enough to be sixteen but still retaining all the best parts of her mother. She liked the person looking back at her. Perhaps this would be the day. A day with an identity she could hold longer than a few minutes no matter who she met. Camryn smiled with forced confidence.

The morning bell rang and Camryn swallowed hard. She paced and waited for the knock on the door. "Please," she whispered. "Please let it be Sela. Please. Today I deserve to get Sela."

One knock, three quick raps, and one knock. She screamed in delight and opened the door to Sela's smile. A quick camera flash momentarily blinded her.

"Ooooo, you look so sharp today," Sela said. "I love the fashion choice. Fuchsia. I didn't know you had it in you." Sela hugged her. "Happy sweet sixteen." She turned the back of the camera around and pointed to the view screen. "Here. This is who you are today. I thought a picture would help you concentrate."

Camryn reached for it and looked at the picture. She hugged the camera to her chest. "That's the best…" She choked on the words. "Thank you."

"That's not all," Sela said. She drew out a gaily-wrapped rectangular box, about the size of her palm. It was topped with a sprig of fern encircled by small gold and silver seven-pointed stars on a string. "Happy Birthday."

Camryn's heart stopped for a moment and her eyes misted. She skimmed the box with her fingers before taking it.

"Don't tell Dr. Frenelli though," Sela said. "We aren't supposed to play favorites with patients."

Camryn swallowed hard. She'd given up on the thought of ever receiving a present again. The Starlight Center allowed family visitations to the patients, but she no longer had any family. She fumbled with the string of stars wrapped multiple times around the package.

Sela surged forward then clasped her hands together in front of her chest. "Just tear it," she said. "Birthday presents are to be torn into with passion, especially sixteenth birthdays."

Camryn attacked the paper then, giggling and ripping and throwing small pieces of paper and stars away from her. She reached for the edges to remove the top of the small, dark brown box and froze. Her hand wouldn't move. Her lungs wouldn't expand. Her eyes held perfectly still as if moving them would unleash the pressure behind them.

"What's wrong?" Sela asked. "It's okay. It won't explode."

"I…it's just that…" Camryn couldn't stop her voice from shaking. "My mother promised me…" She couldn't stop the tears forming. She looked up to Sela's face, unsure whether to open the box—unwilling to face disappointment.

Sela hugged her tight. "It's okay, sweetie. It's just a trinket. I'm sure your mother would approve."

Camryn bit down on her bottom lip. Her face stung as if thousands of small fingers pinched her skin between sharp fingernails. Her hair changed from a curly chestnut to blonde and straight. Her scalp tingled as her hair contracted into a short bob just like Sela's.

"I'm sorry," she apologized, holding the box out to give it back. "I can't help it."

Sela waved her hand and pushed the box back toward Camryn. "You're fine. I take it as a compliment that you look like me." She pointed to the box. "Go on, open it. Take a chance. See if it fits who you want to be."

Camryn slowly raised the lid. Inside was a forest green silken pouch. She loosened the black thong holding it closed at the top and peered inside. It was some type of animal. She reached in to pull it out by the chain attached to it. A small pewter owl, its wings spread in full flight, sat in the palm of her hand. Its talons held a small white orb, and above its head was a crescent moon.

"You've often spoken of the forest and how at home you feel there," Sela said. "I bought this at a myth and magic shop. They told me the white pearl at the bottom held magical powers. The name of this piece is 'Flight of the Goddess for Awareness & Knowledge.' Read the little description on the scroll in the bottom of the pouch."

Camryn pulled out the small piece of paper and unfurled it. She read aloud, "A whisper of shadow, soft wings in the dusk, the owl warns of approaching danger and sharpens inner and outer vision. Under a crescent moon, wise and wild, she flies swift through the Greenwood to capture the truth." She looked up at Sela. Her tongue felt numb in her mouth. She clasped her arms around Sela's waist and held tight.

Sela hugged her back. "You're welcome, sweetie. I know

you're trying hard…trying to find the truth about yourself. Maybe this will help you capture it."

After a few moments Sela let go. "Here, let me put it on you." Camryn handed her the necklace and Sela gestured a circle with her fingers. "Turn around."

Tears temporarily averted, Camryn turned her back and Sela placed the loop around her. The owl hung just below the hollow of her neck, the small pearl warmed against her throat.

"There," Sela said as she secured the clasp. "Let's see."

Camryn turned back and worked on a shaky smile. Her fingers caressed the owl. "Thank you. It's beautiful. It's perfect."

"I think it's a great complement to your outfit." Sela pointed to the picture again still displayed on the back of the camera. "Though I'm flattered you look like me, I liked this identity better though. It had some of your mother, but was still your age. I think you're beginning to choose who you are. Do you want to go back to this?"

Camryn concentrated on the picture and nodded.

"You can do it," Sela encouraged. "Keep looking at the picture. I'll wait."

Camryn shut out everything else in the room except the image in the camera's viewing window. The pricks of pain were not as pronounced this time. She again felt her hair lengthen and return to the wavy chestnut brown she'd started with this morning. Soon she looked up at Sela, her brows raised in question.

"You did it!" Sela clapped and pointed to the mirror. "Go look. And see if you still like your necklace."

Camryn smiled so big her cheeks hurt. She was back to the way she started this morning and she'd done it on her own. This was a good identity. She turned back to Sela. "I want this one," Camryn said. "I want to keep it. Will you print me a picture I can keep with me?"

"Of course, sweetie. I'll get it for you right after breakfast."

Breakfast. Camryn had already forgotten. She was feeling too good right now to go to the cafeteria and be confused by everyone else in the room. "Could you get it now so I can take it to breakfast with me and try to keep it together?"

"Good idea," Sela said. "Sure, I'll be right back." She turned toward the door. As she grasped the handle to walk out, she turned back. "Keep looking in that mirror. When I come back with the picture, I want to see the same person in front of me."

Camryn nodded as Sela closed the door. If she could hang on to this identity, maybe Dr. Frenelli would let her out of Starlight Center when she turned eighteen. Though he'd never believe she could be cured, maybe she could convince him she wasn't a danger to herself or others.

~

CAMRYN HELD the paper and picture in front of her, glancing forward only occasionally as she and Sela made their way toward a table for two. They were running late and, unlike her usual breakfast time, the dining room was filled with patients. She was never allowed to eat at the same time other patients ate. But it was her birthday. Today she was a rebel.

She quickly scanned the room. Most patients sat in small groups with friends. Two orderlies stood in opposite corners, their eyes roving constantly. Sela motioned toward a window. Camryn didn't like windows because sometimes patients would peer into them and that would distract her. However, there didn't appear to be anywhere else available that was just for two. At least the window table was somewhat separated from the others. Clutching the picture with one hand, and Sela's hand with the other, they made their way past several tables in the center. She didn't dare glance at anyone for longer than a few seconds. Never before had she tried to hold a single image for so long. It would be a real test for her to hold it with so many people around.

Finally they sat. She pulled the picture to her face so that it was the only thing she could see. Concentrating, she kept describing herself over and over in a whisper. "Chestnut hair, curly, waist length. Blue eyes. Tan skin. No wrinkles. Five feet, five inches tall, one hundred twenty pounds."

"You're doing great," Sela said. "Hang in there and I'll go get us breakfast. Pancakes or cereal?"

"Cereal…chestnut hair, curly, waist length. Blue eyes. Tan…" Camryn heard the chair scrape as Sela got up but she refused to be distracted. "I won't look. I won't look up," she kept saying to herself while simultaneously reciting her description in her mind.

Someone tapped her shoulder. She glanced up expecting to see Sela. Her breath whooshed from her lungs as she gazed upon what could only be described as a hallucination. Sometimes the drugs Dr. Frenelli prescribed caused her to see things —but usually it was just a kaleidoscope of colors, or objects moving in fast circles around her. With the drugs everything looked like a Monet painting—an impressionist view of the world.

But this wasn't that kind of hallucination. Not at all. The person before her seemed very real, very three-dimensional. He was unlike anyone she'd ever seen. Ebony hair combed straight back from his forehead was styled so perfect it couldn't possibly be real. Its very darkness emphasized piercing grey-blue eyes, shadowed by strong brows that suggested serious competence.

His chiseled jaw line sported a faint beard and mustache. She wasn't sure if he hadn't shaved for a day or two, or if it was his normal look. She stared at him and consciously had to close her mouth. He was like a young version of guys on the cover of romance novels she'd read. He had to be close to her own age though. His skin was smooth.

Darn it! She hadn't had a hallucination for at least a week. She'd thought the drug dosages were worked out now. She closed her eyes, certain that when she opened them again the fantasy man would disappear. She peaked out from under lashes. Nope. Not gone. She closed them again. Not real. Not real. Not real. Men like this only appeared in movies or on TV, not in real life, and he definitely didn't look like any patient she'd ever seen at Starlight Center. Open?

She met his eyes for an instant and then immediately looked away, her breath coming in short pants as she felt the tingle in her scalp, the stretching of her skin. Nooooooo! She focused on her picture. I will not turn into him. I will not turn into him, she chanted in her mind. I am a sixteen-year-old girl. Curly hair, brownish-red, waist length. No, not short. Not short. Below the shoulders. Below the shoulders. Blue eyes, tan skin, five feet five inches…

Though she tried to ignore him, Camryn saw him take the seat opposite her. She pulled the picture into her direct line of sight, blocking any view beyond it.

"Are you Wynbune?" he asked. His accent was strange, and his voice seemed raspy like it was out of practice of making a sound.

"I'm not Win Beyoone," she said. "I've never heard that name. Or is it a state of being? Like crazy? Is it a foreign word for crazy? Because if that's what you're asking. I am definitely crazy." She paused, realizing her words were running away.

"And now I'm talking to a hallucination." She pounded her fist on the table. "Crap. Crap. Crap. This is not good. This is really not good."

He reached for the paper in her hand, but she withdrew it quickly.

He wrapped soft fingers around her wrist—not in a violent way but she was sure she could not move out of their embrace. A comforting warmth spread from his fingers up her arm.

"I know you, Wynbune. I could not be mistaken." He lowered her hand and the paper with it. "I feel the magic in you."

"I have no magic," she said, surprised her voice wasn't shaking. "Let. Me. Go," she said in her most confident voice, even though it was a whisper.

He did not let go. Instead he leaned forward so that she could not ignore him. "I know your secret, Chameleon. I am here to help. I will hold the image for you so you can rest."

She looked at him then and shuddered. For some reason she had no desire to remove her hand. She continued to watch him, to wait for the stings to assail her nerve endings, to wait for when she turned into him, to wait for him to scream and run away. Instead, he continued to sit there, holding her hand, calming her, and she didn't feel anything changing at all. For the first time in her life she wasn't scared. She wasn't ready to run. For the first time in her life she felt completely safe.

She lifted her other hand to her hair and pulled it toward her. Still long and chestnut brown. And wavy. "How?" She asked him. "No one has been able to stop the change. No one."

"Wynbune, I have come to take you away from the Agnoses. To take you home."

"I don't have a home...anymore," she said, her voice a weary whisper. "This is it. Even if they'd let me out I don't know where I'd go."

He relaxed his grip and his thumb stroked the inside of her wrist. "To the forest, Wynbune. I will take you back to the forest."

Okay, this really was crazy. Her hallucinations never touched her. Maybe he was a patient after all. But how would he know her most secret dream? She hadn't told anyone, except Dr. Frenelli.

Ahhhhh. Now she understood. This was a trick. Dr. Frenelli was testing her. He seemed to always be testing her, pushing her. He called it reshaping her reality. Taking away her crutches. Forcing her to live in the normal world.

The young man turned her face back toward him, his palm soft on her cheek. "I see you do not believe me. What must I do to convince you? What test would you ask of me? Whatever it is I will do it."

Ah ha. He said test. It was Dr. Frenelli. Damn. Damn. Damn. This is the most despicable thing he'd pulled yet.

She looked directly into the guy's eyes and made a fist with her hand. "Let. Go. I don't know who you are or why Dr. Frenelli wants to do this. But whatever the reason, I'm not playing. You tell him I'm sick of his damn tests. Now let go!"

"Who is Dr. Frenelli?"

"Yeah, right. As if you didn't know."

He relaxed his grip and she withdrew her hand.

"I am Ohar. I cannot be long from the forest. It pains me not to feel the caress of Mazikeen magic. I do not know how to live among the Agnoses for more than a few days." He stood and it seemed that the rest of the room beyond him blurred. It didn't disappear, it was like a gauzy filter had surrounded them. Only Camryn and Ohar were in sharp relief.

"I have been waiting for you, Wynbune. We all have been waiting. Come outside now and I will help you." He extended his hand to her, palm up as if inviting her to a ballroom dance. "I will help you return to your home in the forest."

Wow. He was good. Very good. She wanted to believe him. Even if just for a moment, a half hour maybe. Would it hurt? Even if it was a test, what did it matter? Maybe Dr. Frenelli would let this little game continue long enough for her to actually get outside. It had been almost a year since she'd inhaled that sweet, musty wood. She would do almost anything to briefly walk among the flowering rhodies covering the ground, or to stand among the ten-foot-tall ferns lining the creeks. Her eyes locked on Ohar, searching for truth. Searching for escape.

"You're changing into me," he whispered. He reached for her and pulled her to stand close to him. "Let me help."

He touched her lightly this time, but she felt the change stop immediately. She retained the identity she'd chosen for today—her sixteenth birthday persona.

His thumb traced her chin, as if he was redrawing her identity for her. "That's better, " he said after what seemed like an eternity of silence. "I've kindled your Mazikeen magic so the changes are not as painful. With practice, you can hold images as long as you need."

Okay. Now that was weird. She stared at this unbelievable, ethereal man in front of her. Was it possible? Could he really help her?

No. She shook her head. Who in their right mind would believe some gorgeous guy could suddenly appear and whisk her away to her beloved forest to live happily ever after? Only the fairy tales her mother told her would be like that.

After a few more moments of silence he spoke again. "Are you ready now, Wynbune? Are you ready to go outside?"

"What do you mean, outside?" Camryn asked. "Outside Starlight Center? I don't know what you've been smoking, but I can't go out and you can't check me out, unless you're a doctor. You wouldn't happen to be a shrink would you?"

He laughed. "I don't shrink anyone, and there is no need for you to be smaller."

"Not small. Shrink! You know psychiatrist. Head doctor. People fixer."

Ohar tilted his head to one side and furrowed his brows. "You are Wynbune. You are the Chameleon. The chosen one."

"Right. Chosen. Like I chose to stay here and have nightmares and be drugged all the time."

He put an arm around her waist and gestured to the room. The blur disappeared and she could see all of it again—even the other patients—but she felt no changes in her body. Her mind was calm. How did he do that?

"You can leave here whenever you want," he said. He moved behind her and whispered over her shoulder into her ear. "You don't belong here. You are not one of the Agnoses. You are Wynbune, the Chameleon. Come with me and your mother's people will help you."

Camryn shook her head again as if shaking it enough would expel the hallucination. She wasn't sure what was happening. Why was she calm? Why wasn't she changing into this guy? Maybe she was in Frenelli's lab. Maybe she was doing one of his tests. She often couldn't remember how she got to the lab or what happened there.

Even if this wasn't one of Dr. Frenelli's tests, she was sane enough to know sixteen-year-old girls don't live in the forest with prince charming and no job or money. Sixteen-year-old girls don't have special powers, and if she could leave anytime she wanted then why had it been so hard for her to hold onto an image until today? Nope. This was one bit of sanity she wouldn't let go. If she did, there was definitely no coming back.

With an audible sigh, Ohar turned her toward him and lifted her chin to align her eyes with his. "I have provided a protection spell for you. Your body is ready for the Kintala. If you don't come soon, even my spell cannot protect you from what will happen."

Camryn took in a deep breath. Her memories of other Frenelli tests were never this clear. He never talked about magic, or protection, or running into the woods. She shook her head to deny the hallucination. In the past month, Frenelli had increased the drugs whenever she was in the lab. They made it harder and harder for her to concentrate, or to remember anything that happened.

"I will wait for you as long as I can. Please, Wynbune, do not let them change you. If you stay, the Agnoses will first kill your sight. Then they will kill your will. Finally, they will kill your spirit. Then you will no longer be Wynbune. You will no longer be able to return to us. I've seen it happen to other Mazikeen. Please, don't wait too long to come with me."

Camryn swallowed and wet her lips to speak, but no sound came out. What did he mean? Who were the Ma-suh-keen? And who were the Ag-no-seez?

"You must come home and fulfill the prophecy," he said. "I have seen Mazikeen children burn bright and die with the force of the Abaddon spreading through the lichen from within. I have seen Mazikeen children captured by Agnoses and lost to us forever. I will not let this happen to you."

She looked closely at him again. He seemed like a normal, but there was something different—something in the way he spoke, the way he sat and stood with perfect yet effortless posture, the way he looked into her eyes. Then there was the fact that as long as he touched her she could keep her own image even though she was staring at him. Really staring.

He released his touch and she felt as if she suddenly stepped into a cold mist. She crossed her arms and tried to rub the heat back into them.

"You are not alone," he said. "Not anymore."

Camryn nodded and her eyes filled with tears. She didn't want him to leave, but she also didn't want to give up what little sanity she had left. She hugged herself tighter, her voice useless as the silence stretched between them.

"I am sorry you were forced to live among the Agnoses for so long." Ohar bent and caressed her cheek. "Your mother did not intend it."

Camryn closed her eyes as warmth spread from her cheek down her neck and covered her shoulders like a comforting sweater that had just come fresh from the dryer. Her shoulders dropped and she released her fear, her questions.

"I can see it has been very hard," he continued. "I do not know how you have managed so long without a teacher. When you are ready, get to the forest and the trees will guide you. Your magic is very strong now."

She opened her eyes and looked up at him, her eyes partly covered by a protective fall of hair. His hand left her cheek and he turned. Unable to trust her senses, Camryn focused on him as he left the room. Though he was obviously walking, his feet seemed to glide an inch above the floor. With each step he took away, a bit of warmth bled from her. When she could no longer see him she shuddered with cold.

"It's my birthday," Camryn whispered, her voice more full of tears than her eyes. "I must not cry on my birthday."

THE PLAN

Camryn clutched the picture in front of her and chanted the image she wanted to maintain. She was convinced Ohar had been some type of drug-induced hallucination. What was taking Sela so long? If Sela had been here she could verify whether the man had been real. She dared to glance away for a moment and scanned the cafeteria.

A woman stepped directly into her line of sight and challenged her with her eyes. The woman's bright red hair—a color not found in nature—was shaved on the sides with the center sticking straight up two to three inches as if it could slice anything that came in contact with it. "Who are you?" the woman shouted. "Who are you?"

Camryn froze. Everyone else in the dining hall stopped talking as the woman shrieked at her. "You dare to sit at my table?"

Each word sounded an alarm in Camryn's head. The woman's piercing wail sucked all light from the room, leaving only an inky black fear. She knew her control was slipping.

There was nothing she could do except hang on to her sides, trying to stop the gnawing of her stomach as she changed.

"The picture, Camryn!" She heard Sela's voice as if it was clouded in a heavy storm, blown from far away. "The picture!" But it was too late.

"A witch," the woman's voiced pierced the veil as she backed away.

A cacophony of steps and screams swirled around the dining room. Camryn looked to one side, to get the woman's face out of her mind. She saw a man with a burn from his chin to cheekbone, his blonde hair cut so that it somewhat obscured it. She quickly looked away. Too late. He screamed and ran, and she knew she had now taken on his image.

Patients ran in all directions shouting, "Witch! Demon! Satan!"

Camryn struggled to stand. She had to leave the room. She didn't know where she was. She struggled to keep her balance, moving from one table to another as the changes accelerated. She could no longer keep track. The colors. The sounds. The movement.

"Camryn!" She recognized Sela's voice. "Look at me, Camryn." Hands shook her shoulders. "Look at me! It's okay. I'm here. Look at me."

She turned in Sela's direction and took refuge in her embrace, glad to take on the image of someone she knew. Someone who wouldn't be frightened. Someone who wouldn't scream or run.

"Clear the room now!" Dr. Frenelli's voice commanded.

Orderlies rushed in the doors and dealt with struggling patients, moving them back to their rooms.

Camryn tensed as she peeked above Sela's arm toward Frenelli.

His scrunched eyes and wrinkled nose capped his pursed mouth as if he'd just sucked in vinegar. "How dare you bring her to breakfast at this hour," Frenelli said. "She is only to go for meals in off hours. You know that. You know the rules. It will take us hours to calm everyone down." He motioned to two orderlies the size of NFL linemen.

They pried her away from Sela's embrace.

"No!" Sela said, still squeezing Camryn's hand, refusing to let go. "Leave her alone. I'll take her. I'll take her back to her room."

One of the orderlies pried Sela's fingers off Camryn's hand, and with one sharp jerk the other orderly had distanced Camryn from her by at least five feet.

"You've done enough damage," Frenelli said between closed teeth and a snarl. "You know this is a special client, with special rules. I will have to report this and she may be moved to another facility. Is that what you want?"

Sela backed away from Camryn and silently mouthed *sorry*. "No. No, I…"

"Your shift is over." Frenelli wrote something on a prescription pad and slapped it against Sela's chest. "Tomorrow you will pick up your final paycheck. This is inexcusable. I knew your getting close to this child would eventually wreak havoc. You've ruined months of research, set her recovery back to zero. Now go! Go before you do any more damage."

Camryn kicked back against the human bulwark that held her. He yelped and the second orderly grabbed her legs and held them up, suspending her between the two men. She squirmed and tried to kick out of their hold.

"No! I want Sela! It's not her fault. It's mine. It's my birthday. Don't you understand? She was just being nice. Please, it's my birthday!" She couldn't hold back the tears. What had she done?

What had she done to the only person who truly cared about her in this awful place?

She felt a prick on her arm. "This will calm you," Frenelli said. "It will stop the changes for now." He nodded at the two men holding her. "You can stand her up. She won't fight you." Then he turned and forcibly escorted Sela from the room.

One of the goons said, "Are you going to walk or shall we carry you all the way?"

"I'll… walk," Camryn choked on a sob. "Please, put me down. I'll walk."

They flanked her at either side as she mechanically put one foot in front of the other, each step seeming further from her consciousness. She hated this drugged state. This was why she never interacted with other patients. Dr. Frenelli would love to keep her drugged all the time. He didn't want to help her learn how to control the changes at all. He just wanted them stopped —stopped so she would be stuck with whatever image she last had. She'd show him. She'd learn to change into him and then see if he screamed and ran. Right now, she was still the image of Sela. She hoped she could keep it, if for no other reason than to piss off Frenelli. Blonde hair. A bob. She recited Sela's image to herself making sure everyone knew this was who she cared about. This was who she chose to be.

Every time she saw Frenelli in the future she would be sure to look like Sela. She vowed her vengeance on Dr. Frenelli. She would make sure he would never be rid of Sela's image.

She stumbled against one of the goons and shuddered as she drew herself inward, trying to make everything as small as possible, trying to make sure there was no reason for either of them to touch her.

Focused on placing one foot in front of the other, looking only at the ground, she counted as her mother had taught her—

counted to keep herself calm. It was four hundred and eighty-three steps from the dining hall to the south wing of Starlight Center. Then it was another two hundred and twenty-seven paces to the corridor of individual rooms. Then up exactly nine steps to the second floor and a left turn. She counted every step, and looked at no one. Outside of her ballet flats, all she saw were the four large feet in sturdy black shoes that walked beside her.

By the time she reached her room, Camryn found that any small joy to be had from her birthday was gone, extinguished first by terror and now by mind-numbing drugs. The lock clicked and she was finally alone in her room. Camryn shuffled to her bed, wavered, then melted onto the sheets.

The sob exploded taking all air with it, and she sunk into a storm of confusion. She gasped to breathe, repeatedly fighting back to the surface, only to be swamped again as the flood of hopelessness lured her back down. She curled into a tight ball, her hands fisted over her heart, their pressure a counterbalance to the weight threatening to stop its beat. As each thud crashed against the wall of her chest, it hammered one more nail of desperation, one more nail of despair into the coffin that trapped her—Starlight Center.

CAMRYN WOKE FROM A DREAMLESS SLEEP, her body stiff from not changing positions. She uncoiled her legs and tentatively stretched, pointing her toes hard. She consciously lowered her shoulders and rolled onto her stomach. Pushing with her forearms she arched her back and stretched like a cat after a long nap. The clock on the bedstand read 6:45. A new day. A new plan.

A week of routine and meeting with Dr. Frenelli daily since her birthday had hardened her resolve to do something... anything other than continue one more day at Starlight Center. For over a year she'd been the quiet, shy, young woman accepting her doomed fate—doing whatever the doctors and nurses asked of her, searching for normal, hoping to fit in or at least fake it. But Sela had shown her she could be something more. She could be whoever she wanted.

Sela had been the only one who understood Camryn, the only one who truly cared. She'd taught Camryn how to pretend to take the drugs but not swallow. She'd reinforced her mother's teachings on how to get through by counting—counting steps, counting seconds, counting minutes, counting days. Now that Sela was gone, there was no reason to stay. No reason to play Dr. Frenelli's games anymore. No reason to try to become normal.

Every day since Sela left, she'd met Dr. Frenelli in Sela's image. In spite of his attempts to force her to change, to scare her back to her old ways, she'd refused. Of course, she didn't know what happened when she was so drugged she couldn't remember. But each night, when an orderly returned her to her room she would change into her own identity—the one Sela had helped her to form.

Camryn had hidden the picture in her room in a vent no one would ever search. She took it out each night and reminded herself who she'd chosen to be that day. Camryn could now put on her chosen identity whenever she wanted. The identity she'd chosen for herself. The identity she would wear after she left Starlight Center.

The thought of escape gave Camryn enough strength to get off the bed. In the secret of her room, before the shift change each morning, she'd been practicing how to change into Dr. Frenelli. She'd worked her way up from holding his image for a few minutes to an entire hour. If everything went according to plan, she only needed to hold Dr. Frenelli's identity inside her for fifteen minutes. Just long enough for her to escape.

She pulled on black pants and a white top. They somewhat matched Dr. Frenelli's usual attire. He always wore a white shirt and tie, covered by a pullover sweater. He favored the sweater instead of a suit jacket—thinking it made him appear younger, friendlier. Right. As if a skinny, short, white-haired, sixty-year-old stick in the mud could ever appear friendly.

She slipped on the pullover sweater she'd stolen from Frenelli's office after a particularly awful session where she shook in fear for at least an hour after coming off the drugs. The sweater was a little heavy and stiff. She sneezed at the clinging smell of moth balls. Why did he keep it in there if he never wore it?

When her arms were through, the sweater easily covered most of her blouse. She pulled it down to hang just below the waistline of her pants.

A tie. Dr. Frenelli always wore a tie. She needed something muted she could use to fake a tie around her neck. For a moment she fingered the scarves she had in her drawer, knowing she would never see them again. She would be leaving with just the clothes on her back. She couldn't walk out with a big suitcase and still pretend to be Dr. Frenelli. Even if she looked like him, he would never carry a suitcase.

She dug further in the shoebox of scarves. A narrow cotton print she used to wear as a headband lay below the pink silk. The blue background with white polka dots just might be enough to fool someone. It was a little too bright for Dr. Frenelli, but with most of it covered by the sweater she might get away with it—especially if she could lift a lab coat from one of the staff.

Camryn looked down at the outfit she had assembled so far. Her shoes! Dr. Frenelli definitely wouldn't be caught wearing ballet slippers with flowers. She dug into her closet and found the one pair of boots she'd brought with her. The dark leather with a rounded toe didn't match his usual staid oxfords, but most people didn't look at feet. They looked at your face—that is everyone except Camryn.

This would be a real test for her—keeping an image of Dr. Frenelli for long enough to walk out of the building. She'd have to make sure she didn't really look at anyone—didn't notice much about them. Focus. Focus. Focus.

She had to do it. Her life depended on it. She could no longer stay here or she would certainly die. She couldn't remember most of her sessions with Frenelli. She only knew when she came out of the drugs she was exhausted and often had to be carried back to her room. Something wasn't right. It felt like she was getting weaker instead of stronger from Frenelli's therapy.

Isn't that what Ohar told her? The guy she still wasn't sure if he was a hallucination or not. He said she would lose her will and then she would lose her soul. She took a deep breath. If they caught her what would happen? Would they shoot? Or would they simply give her enough drugs to kill her?

Camryn looked around the room one last time. The dream-catcher! She reached over the bed and removed it from the wall. It was the only thing she had left of her parents. She had to find a way to take it with her. It wasn't that big—maybe the size of a dessert plate. She stuffed it partially down her pants, then tucked in her shirt and pulled the sweater back over. It wasn't comfortable but it would keep her walking stiffly, like Frenelli always did.

Determined, she marched to the mirror and prepared herself. She focused on becoming Dr. Frenelli. First the hair. His was definitely white with a receding hairline, a little shaggy in the back falling on his collar, but the sides were trimmed close with his ears prominent on the sides of his head. With her practice every day this week, she knew what to expect. The stings of electricity along her scalp barely hurt anymore. Next, her cheeks and chin pulled and stretched as a white beard and mustache appeared. She focused the pain on a bald spot on either side of his goatee where no hair grew. It was as if frowning so often made sure hair wouldn't grow there. She gasped and sucked on her cheeks to allay the stiffness and ache left from the transformation.

His nose was fairly angular, of normal size but with a definite thinness which also helped to emphasize his prominent cheekbones and the sunken look of his cheeks that were not fully covered by his beard. Her sinuses suddenly felt stuffed as if she had a cold. She snuffed in a breath. She needed more wrinkles around the eyes. She drew her finger across her forehead to work out a big crease just above the brows. Her head ached with the squeeze of pressure and she rubbed her temples for relief.

Camryn looked at her hands. Definitely needed some age spots and the beginnings of arthritis. Her fingers stiffened. Done. She felt old, sad, every part of her ached. The waking bell rang and she continued to stand in front of the mirror, focusing, concentrating on Frenelli's image, waiting for someone to fetch her for breakfast. Yes. This was good. It should be enough to get her out the door.

Bam. Bam. Bam. The heavy knock was definitely not one of

the female nurses. She cleared her throat. "Get in here now," she shouted in Frenelli's voice. "You idiot, get in here now!"

The door cracked and one of the football-type orderlies peered in.

She stomped to the door and threw it open wide. Shaking her fist, she scrunched her face and set her jaw, speaking through her teeth as she'd seen Dr. Frenelli do many times. "She tricked me and locked me in here," she said. "Don't just stand there, find her! Find her and bring her to my office. Start with the dining room. If she's not there, search every room. We are going to end this irresponsibility once and for all. She's not to be trusted. She's not to be allowed near the other patients."

The goon did a double-take, as if ensure it was really Frenelli.

"Don't stand there, man. Move!" Camryn yelled again in Frenelli's voice and pushed at the orderly's chest.

The goon took a minute to react, but he seemed to finally accept what his eyes told him and he turned and ran out of the room.

Camryn slipped into the hall, closed the door silently behind her, and stepped in the opposite direction. Straightening her shoulders, she adopted the confident gait of Dr. Frenelli. As she passed the staff lounge, she noticed a white lab coat hanging on a hook with no one there to claim it. She moved inside and donned it instantly.

It was strange walking toward the front door with no one in sight. She'd timed it perfectly. At 7:30 the staff were only half an hour into the shift change. It was likely the nurses were still reviewing charts and setting up their work for the day—not really paying much attention to anyone else. At the point where she reached the lobby, she nodded briefly to the receptionist who smiled at her.

"Forget something, doctor?" the young woman asked.

Camryn nodded. "My car. I'll be just a moment," she answered, her voice an exact duplicate of Frenelli's.

"Stop!" Frenelli yelled from behind her. "That's the patient. Stop her!"

The orderly she'd sent from her room grabbed her roughly.

"What are you doing?" she demanded. "I'm Frenelli." She pointed at Frenelli. "That's Camryn Painter. Can't you tell by the way she is slightly bent over? I don't walk like that. Look at how red she's getting. That's her anger taking over. She's going to go bezerk at any moment. Take her back to her room. Now!"

The orderly looked at her and then at Frenelli.

Frenelli stepped forward and grabbed her other arm. "This is the patient," he said again. This time he had more control of his emotions. "Look at the pants. Those are Starlight Center issued pants. Look at the shoes. Have you ever seen me wear boots?"

Don't panic. Don't panic.

Camryn stared hard at the orderly. Within seconds she grew another foot taller and gained at least 50 pounds, her clothes split at the seams as she changed.

The orderly screamed and dropped his hold on her.

Camryn ran for the door.

"Stop her!" Frenelli screamed. "The emergency locks. Activate them."

She didn't look back. Her arms hit the bar on the door and she barreled through. She heard the locks snick into place and Frenelli's frustrated scream demanding they open the door again.

Her feet pounded the asphalt hard as she ran toward the forest. She had to put as much space as possible between her and Frenelli's goons. She had maybe a minute, tops, before the emergency locks could be opened again.

She hit the first set of trees and headed downhill, her lungs worked hard as her leg muscles strained against the grade making sure she didn't fall. One thing she remembered from living in the forest is that going downhill you would eventually hit water. She hoped it would be soon—a creek, a stream, anything to cover her tracks.

When she'd first arrived at Starlight Center she'd heard the story of a patient who tried to escape. They sent dogs after him. Though she'd never seen him, the rumor was that the dogs killed him.

The alarm sounded for miles around—the emergency door had unlocked. The alarm alerted anyone in the area that a crazy person was loose and to lock their doors. No one would help her now. She was on her own.

She ran faster. There had to be a stream. *Please, let there be a stream—a waterfall, the ocean—anything.* She wasn't picky. She didn't want to be killed by dogs. She didn't want to be killed at all.

THE ESCAPE

Camryn ran without stopping for several minutes, until she was well hidden in a cathedral of trees. Gasping for air, she stripped off the argyle sweater and it's hot confinement. Her breathing slowed as the light breeze rippled through the trees and cooled her. Then she reached for the dreamcatcher still stuffed in her waistband. It had rubbed against her skin every step. She took the looped hanger and dropped it over her head to wear like a necklace. It hung just below the owl pendant Sela had gifted her.

Sela. Camryn gulped back the combination of grief and self-blame as she remembered her part in getting Sela fired. She closed her eyes and remembered the picture Sela had made for her, and concentrated on returning to the one and only identity she'd ever chosen for herself. Much more quickly than ever before, back came the chestnut curls. Though she had no mirror with her, she was confident the tanned skin and the youthful appearance returned as well. She was back! She was free!

Then Camryn sobered. She'd escaped, but that was as far as her plan had gone. Now what? The forest had always been her friend. Growing up she'd climbed the trees in her backyard whenever she was scared or sad. She'd spent several nights at the top of the oak near her home when her parents hadn't returned. She had taken many hikes into the redwoods with her family. In fact, they'd hiked and camped there so often that she considered it her personal backyard.

For what seemed like the millionth time she wondered if that guy—Ohar—had been real. What had he said? Go to the forest and it will guide you. Was it possible? She turned in a circle and looked for a sign. She walked fifty feet in one direction, then backtracked and went 50 feet in the opposite direction. She stopped and listened, all her senses straining for anything, any sign. There was nothing.

A breeze ruffled her long hair and she sighed. Of course he wasn't real. For the past week she'd figured Ohar was a hallucination. Some waking dream brought on by the drugs Dr. Frenelli always forced on her. She must have let the sense of freedom get to her. Fantasy and magic weren't real. She was on her own. No counting on someone to save her. Besides, she didn't leave Starlight Center because of Ohar. She left for herself. It was time to find out if she truly had a gift or was doomed to forever be a freak.

She wrapped her arms around her chest and hugged herself. She'd done it! She was free. She no longer had the weight pressing on her chest like it had every day for the past year. She breathed in the fresh air of the forest. She didn't need Ohar. She didn't need anybody but herself.

With new confidence she wrapped the arms of the sweater around her waist and moved further into the forest. At first her steps were uneven as she walked over the ground of forest litter and large roots. As the grove grew denser, she would take a little zig and then pull herself around a big tree and take a zag. Not a direct route, but a path searching for some sign to set her direction. Even a narrow deer path would be welcome right now, something she could begin to navigate before nightfall.

For the first hour she stopped several times to listen, to check, to make sure no one was following. She tracked the position of the sun whenever she'd come into a small clearing. After what felt like a couple hours with no one in pursuit she figured she was safe and could rest. She rolled her shoulders and then her head to relax. Leaning her face against a giant tree, she put her hands out to each side and hugged it.

For Camryn, the redwoods had always been special. Rooted for centuries, the living wood grew tall and thickened with a hundred thousand days of light, and somehow she knew deep inside they were offering her a home, maybe the only home she would have for a long time.

After several more zigzag legs of hiking, she decided her best bet was to climb straight uphill. Maybe at the top she could get her bearings and find a good place to spend the night before dark. She grimaced as she started to climb. Her calf muscles, no longer used to long hikes, were already protesting. Camryn alternately gripped smaller tree trunks and wild rhododendron bushes, pulling herself along when the climb became too steep to use only her legs. As was her habit, she started counting steps, the regular rhythm temporarily banishing the mental images of running into cougars or bears—or even taking a slide on slippery moss and falling down an endless slope until she hit a tree and knocked herself unconscious.

She hardly noticed the light waning as she walked through the now fog-shrouded redwood grove. Sounds were reduced to the musical gurgle of water trickling amongst ferns and mossy rocks. Light ebbed with the somber mist, and shafts of sun hung like cobwebs. Her own pale shadow disappeared as night fell. Stillness and peace wove a spell around her until she felt cocooned in the comforting arms of darkness.

When Camryn could no longer see enough to walk she stopped and counted her breaths, encouraging her heart to slow. She closed her eyes and opened all her other senses. Something moved nearby. A howl. Coyotes hunting prey. The grass in a meadow answered the wind. Then silence. Camryn held her breath.

Two hoots. Her breath whooshed out and she opened her eyes just in time to duck as an owl flew right past her head. Absently, she fingered the owl pendant about her neck. Was it only a week ago that Sela had given it to her? What was it the small scroll said? The owl warns of approaching danger and sharpens inner and outer vision.

Danger! She heard the distant tromping of feet somewhere below where she stood. Certainly Dr. Frenelli wouldn't send people out in the darkness for her. She would not let them take her back. She squeezed her eyes closed and looked for that inner vision. She wasn't sure if she believed, but she needed something right now.

When next she opened them, a faint, sparkly light dappled lichen on rocks and logs near her. The luminous lichen spread from the forest floor and slowly traced a path among the ferns pointing Camryn due north from her current position. As she moved forward, the lighted lines behind her faded. With each step, another ten to twenty feet would be lit, then again fade as she passed. She was not on any normal trail, yet the lights led her among the tall trees in a way so as not to have her tripping over roots, fallen logs, or sliding into a canyon of ferns.

With each step Camryn felt her breath enter and leave her

mouth. As she passed each tree along the faintly lit path, it seemed that she could hear the tree's blood pulsing through veins with the same life-giving oxygen that suffused her own body. Then the path quickly climbed into a cathedral grove, where eight redwoods guarded a small waterfall as it fell into an inviting pool. She wanted to stop and feel the water welcoming her home, but she knew it was too cold at this hour. The lights led her beyond the pool, climbing another forty feet or so to the top of the falls, to a small stream which flowed between steep green banks of lighted ferns.

The trail turned and climbed again, steeply up a ridge into a meadow that was so protected from the night it almost felt warm. Here the lichen was so profuse that the perfect crystalline green and white lights of the trees and ferns along the path put all the area in bright relief. She was no longer sure if she was dreaming while walking, or if she'd discovered some new type of firefly—ones that traveled in groups along lichen. She shook a nearby vining maple, but the lights didn't move. Nothing flew off. She turned in a circle and the lights seemed all around her. They were so bright that she thought for a moment she might have hiked through the night and into the dawn of the next day. But beyond the circle it was still dark.

Camryn struggled to keep her eyes open. As if knowing she needed sleep, the lights in the meadow dimmed along a path pointing to a lone oak in the midst of the redwood grove. She leaned against the trunk, wrapping her arm around a lower branch. Could she sleep standing up? No. Not safe. Too many animals prowl the forest. Especially at night.

A broken lower branch provided just the right foothold to lift her into the tree. She stepped onto it and pulled herself up, grabbing the next higher branch, and the next one. After ascending seven or eight more branches she secured a place in a notch between the trunk and a strong branch that extended over the meadow. She nestled further into the crook and made sure she could balance well. From where she sat, she could survey almost a full circle without much effort. Her eyes tracked back the way she had come. It was complete darkness. She couldn't make out any part of the trail she had followed. The lack of any reflection reinforced it was still night despite the brightness at this particular spot. She held her breath and listened, hoping whoever had been following before was now lost or had given up. She heard nothing except the occasional croak of a tree frog and the skitter of a squirrel.

The meadow was just as brightly lit as before. Even the warmth she had felt on the ground seemed to reach up the tree, as if embracing her and protecting her from the cold. It was as if this lone oak formed a gateway to something else. Strange that it was here, so prominent among the giant redwoods. She shook her head. That was silly. A gateway? What tale of her mother's was she remembering now? Where else could she be except in the same redwood forest she had entered early this morning?

Camryn glanced forward and the lights in the meadow dimmed with her movement. It appeared that the trail became more gentle there, no more climbing.

Tender stalks of grass lined each side and a variety of mush-rooms and other fungus stood bright orange and yellow against the green, as if mimicking the display of wild flowers that would be a part of other forests. Her stomach grumbled, reminding her she'd left without food. Dark with moisture, she wondered if these mushrooms were the type you could eat. No, she couldn't chance it. Getting sick while others may still be hunting her was not a wise plan. She'd gone without food for several days when her parents had died before returning to the house for something to eat. Certainly one or two nights in the forest were not going to kill her.

Her eyes felt heavy. Pulling the sweater from around her waist, she formed it into a pillow and placed it in the tree nook to comfort her head. Just a little nap is all she needed. Maybe twenty minutes and she would feel renewed. Yes, just a few minutes, maybe an hour. No more.

~

OHAR STRUGGLED through the seasonal stream as he followed the trail over yet another sloping ridge. Early this morning, the trees had begun to sing, announcing the moment the Chameleon entered the forest and he was nowhere near to help her.

He'd waited for Wynbune for a week and when she did not appear he'd questioned his vision. Perhaps she was not the one the Mazikeen grandmothers had foretold. She'd seemed so unsure, so dispirited when he'd left her at Starlight Center. He'd thought surely he'd failed. And when she didn't show one day after the next, he knew he'd have to report back to the council. He'd have to dash all the hopes that had traveled with him. The burden was so heavy he'd followed the forest canopy to the ocean to cleanse his guilt and to ask forgiveness from the sea before returning to the Mazikeen. He should have stayed. He should have trusted the prophecy.

Now it was dark and Ohar had to rely on the forest to guide him to her. He knew the moment she re-entered the forest, she would start through the change—the Kintala. At first she would notice nothing different, but with each day it would become more difficult for her to walk until the Kintala was complete. Without a guide she could become lost and hurt herself. Or worse, incapacitated she could be taken by a Boha'a thief or lured by the Abaddon. None of the Mazikeen had been through the Kintala without a guide and lived. Now the Chameleon was lost—probably scared. Maybe…no he refused to think it. If she had already died certainly they would know. Certainly, the forest would have wept.

At 1,000 feet, the trail turned eastward to follow the rim of the fern canyon. Though he couldn't see it, he could hear the crash of waves in the ocean. Without sight, the sea seemed to have risen, as if the waves would catch him even at this elevation. He peered behind him. The stream flowed from the canyon making its way to the sea. Though he couldn't follow it with his eyes in this darkness, he knew the path led back to the source. The center of all the connected redwoods, the place where the Chameleon would undergo her change.

Finally, cresting the next ridge he was able to see more in the moonlight. Now that he was out from the canopy of trees he could follow the ridge marked by a line of spruce, standing like flags in the sea wind. The ridge dipped down into another canyon, and then the trail rose again more steeply. Here the boughs of a tall fir draped across the trail. A litter of spent pine branches and cones softened the steep hillside. A moss covered wall on the uphill side of the trail led him between groves of redwoods and stands of tan oaks, and open places where the fresh leaves of wild iris pushed aside the debris of the past season.

Around each bend he could see the summit of the final ridge coming closer.

The trail wound through a series of switchbacks to the east and south, sending him deeper and deeper into the darkness of the tall trees—the old growth now beckoned him. The trail hooked east again and finally he saw the open meadow below him, alight with the gateway source. He stopped for a moment and smiled. She was here. The Chameleon had found her way home. He listened, expecting to hear Wynbune's laugh or to see her dancing in the center of the meadow, but he heard nothing.

Ohar frowned. Where was she? She must be near or the meadow would not be lit. He stopped and listened again. He was almost afraid to move forward—afraid that he would somehow change the prophecy by entering this sacred area without her. After several minutes he found the courage to step out. The meadow soil was tender. It sank under his weight. He walked a few paces then heard the swoop of an owl as it alighted from the lone oak across the glen. Yes, the owl would protect her. How did Wynbune know to befriend the owl when no one had told her?

He moved again, as silently as possible until he was beneath the oak. He looked up to see the owl had returned and perched on the branch above her—keeping a silent vigil while she slept curled into the trunk of the tree. Her head rested on some mound of material, a jacket or sweater of some kind, and her arms dangled beside her. A vine had stretched around her waist, securing her to the branch so she would not fall. Ohar wondered how she knew to trust the tree. Was it possible it was instinctual, even though she was separated from her magic at birth?

Ohar dropped his small pack of bread and berries to the ground, and stooped to sit beside it. He would rest too.

As he slipped into sleep his dreams were troubled. He saw the Pacific as a shimmering lake of fire. The whales still swam there, but they struggled to breathe. The fire upon the sea was constant. He could discern no movement of the swells. Although a pattern was visible, it seemed to be a standing pattern, without motion, and not connected in any way with time. The fire was not engaged with life, it offered only death, as it waited to devour all that swam in the sea.

He shook in his sleep and his chest clamped down on his heart. The hairy one imprisoned by the Mazikeen had warned them of the power of the Abaddon. He said the fire of the seas would devour the water and turn the forest into a sea of ice. Only his daughter, the Chameleon, would have the power to change it. If she understood her power, she could change the energy of time and return the forest to balance.

From within the gateway tree, the prophecy said the Chameleon would pass beyond the space-time dimension into the multiverse of the forest itself. Through the pulsing blood of lichen she would commune with the stars, and time would change to reveal the soul of the universe found in the scattering of light between the stars. Under her watchful eye, the Chameleon could command the pattern of the wind, the force of the sea, and the sun itself would be reflected through her light-drinking eyes to warm the earth once more. That is, if the Abaddon did not steal her first, if Ohar could help her through the change, if…she didn't die.

RETURN TO THE FOREST

Camryn startled awake as she felt a beating of feathers about her head. The owl immediately flew off. She looked above to watch its direction, but the canopy of trees obscured its flight and she lost it. The pale glow of dawn greeted her and she stretched stiff muscles.

"Ow!" she fell through two branches then slapped her hands out to grab the next one. A shower of leaves rained below her. "Darn it!" She wrapped her leg around the branch and pulled herself upright again.

"Good morning, Wynbune." A familiar voice greeted her.

She trembled slightly when she saw the stranger who had met her at the Starlight Center standing below. Had her hallucinations returned or was he real? For a second, her hand twitched on the branch, searching for something to protect herself. She didn't have a knife to cut the branch for a weapon. Last night she had blindly followed the lights without thinking. She just wanted to get away from those searching for her.

Somehow, perhaps stupidly, the lights gave her a feeling of safety and protection.

"There is nothing to fear, Wynbune. It is Ohar. I told you I would be ready to help. Why did you not wait for me after entering the forest?"

"You didn't make sense," she said, a little miffed. "And my name is not Wynbune."

"You are the Chameleon, are you not? Your given name is Wynbune, from the ancient language of the forest people."

"My name is Camryn. As for being a chameleon, I guess I am but not because I want to be." She wished she had a mirror. She wondered who she looked like right now. She looked at her hands, wiggling the slender fingers. At least it appeared that she was still female. Was it possible she had maintained the identity even in her sleep?

"Please come down." He held up his pack. "I have fresh berries and bread for breakfast. Surely you are hungry. Come down and we can talk."

She made her way down the tree, keeping a close eye on him —ready to scamper back to the highest possible branch if he made any untoward movement in her direction.

He smiled and backed away, then turned to open his pack. "You look like the same girl I first approached a week ago. Have you kept your identity with you all this time?"

Inside her heart jumped with happiness. She had woken with that same visage! Though she had been keeping the identity during the day this past week, she had not managed to keep it through the night at Starlight Center. It seemed she'd always awake with whatever was the last person she saw in a dream. Was it simply a matter of wanting a particular image so much that she could make it happen?

She shook her head. Even if it was, she was still unsure who she really should be. This was still a made up version—a conglomeration of her mother and a young girl she'd met in passing. Her eyes watered for a moment as she worried about poor Sela. She'd been her only friend and now she was out of a job—maybe even blacklisted from nursing. She vowed that she would return to search for Sela and make sure she was okay. Somehow she would make it right in the end.

Finally, she lowered herself the last few feet and nervously touched the ground. Her curiosity about Ohar and the sweet treat he held out to her was tempered by the need to be wary of strangers. He looked different than when she'd met him previously. He was younger than she remembered. She'd thought he would be too old for her, but now he seemed closer to her age and not as ethereal. Of course, who knows if the drugs Dr. Frenelli regularly gave her made everyone seem different at Starlight Center.

Ohar was now somewhat intimidating, larger than she remembered from before, and more peculiarly dressed. He seemed to have replaced the casual pants and shirt of the previous visit with a look that was a cross between Robin Hood and a hippie hiker. He wore tights cut off at the ankles, or perhaps they were more like leggings, of camo green. His feet were shod with only river sandals. His khaki, oversized shirt draped to just above his knees and reminded her of something a pirate would wear. Made of some sort of loose cotton jersey, it was belted at the waist with a twisted leather cord. He also sported a large hunting knife in a scabbard on one hip.

He offered her a torn piece of bread with a few berries. "Please. Eat. You will need your strength for our journey."

As she moved closer to take the treat, she noticed the vee of his shirt revealed more of his neck and chest. He wore some type of pendant held by a leather strap. Her forehead puckered as she tried to see the pendant without being too obvious that she was staring at his chest. The metal was similar to the one Sela had given her as a gift, but it was very strange. Where her own was obviously an owl in flight, his was an old man with a beard—but not quite a normal man. The man's hair was made of leaves, and out of the top of his head grew antlers or multiple horns. Below the beard was some type of intricate woven pattern.

Ohar's lips quirked up and he lifted it toward her. "Herne the Hunter," he said.

She looked away quickly, her cheeks warmed at being caught staring at his chest. "It's … unusual," she finally said when she was able to turn back to him.

"The pendant is in the same tradition as yours. When I saw your owl, I knew you were the one—the Chameleon—the one prophesied to fight the Abaddon. We were born to be together."

"Whoa! Hold on. A little necklace given to me as a gift by someone you've never met does not mean we're going to get married, or even grow to like each other." Though as she said it, a small part of her brain was thinking she could really like this guy, and let's face it there hadn't been any other boys interested in her. Not that she'd ever spent more than five minutes with a boy. Turning into the person she sees was never a welcome trick on a first date.

She bit her lower lip. This may be the closest to a second date she'd ever get. "I'm sorry…again. It seems I have a habit of thinking out loud with you. I wasn't saying I didn't want you. I mean….not that I'm saying I do want you…I mean…this just isn't turning out right no matter what I say. The point is that just because we both happened to get a similar gift of these metal pendants doesn't mean we're a love match."

He pulled his shoulders back and puffed out his chest,

pointing to his pendant with a stiff finger. "This was earned. Awarded to me as a member of the true Forest People. Awarded to me for saving the life of…" He suddenly clamped his mouth closed.

"Saving the life of who?"

"It is too early yet," he said, offering her another piece of bread. "You are not yet through the change. You will learn it in time."

She took the bread and bit off a chunk of it, chewing slowly as she pondered why he so suddenly stopped in his story. What kind of strange mystery surrounded this man? For that matter, her whole darn life.

Unwilling to give up, she decided she would take a different route. She pointed to his pendant. "What does it mean? Half man, half animal?"

Ohar bowed his head, carefully not meeting her gaze. She saw that he seemed embarrassed now to speak of his award. "Am I not supposed to ask?" she said. "I don't know your customs. I apologize if I've offended you."

"No, it's fine." He scuffed a foot in the leafy path and then stood tall again, his shoulders back. "I can speak of it. I just don't…I feel…it is like bragging."

She smiled. "Oh, well…you don't have to…I just wondered."

"It is the symbol of the horned hunter, who is one of mystical strength and honor." He quickly spoke the words as if laboring over them would make her ask too many questions. "It means justice and respect. I am chosen to uphold the order of things, to play fair."

She smiled. "Now that wasn't so hard, was it?"

"No," he affirmed, seeming to fight a smile as his cheek dimpled.

Camryn laughed. Ohar's brows lifted in question.

"If you are chosen to be just, to play fair, then you must help me by preparing me for the change, right? You would not leave me to learn on my own and be defeated. Right?"

Ohar stood slowly and looked from one side of the forest to the other, as if there was something or someone out there to answer for him. But he said nothing.

"What am I to learn? What change?" she finally asked.

"I cannot tell you yet."

"But that's not fair, and you're duty bound to be fair."

"You are trying to confuse me," he said. "It is true I am bound to be fair, but I am also bound not to lead you to a decision you may not be ready to make. They are two duties that may seem in conflict but are not. I am clear on what I need to do. And right now I must not reveal too much."

She took in a deep breath and let it out loudly. Crossing her arms across her chest she turned her back to him. "Fine. Don't tell me," she said. "It's not as if I would understand it anyway. It's not as if I want to know why my life is so screwed up. Why I'm a chameleon. Why I'm sitting here eating bread and berries with a stranger in the middle of the forest. No, it's not as if I deserve any answers. Fine. Just fine. I don't want to know anyway. Keep your little secrets. Just see if I…"

Ohar laughed out loud, stopping her in her small tantrum.

"Does that usually work?" he asked.

She turned back around. "Does what work?"

"Putting blame on someone else for your problems. Playing the victim."

She wrinkled her forehead and pursed her lips. No one had ever called her out on that before. "Hmmm. I guess I was. But you have to admit, it's not fair keeping me in the dark."

He shook his head and offered her his hand. "We need to get going."

She let him pull her to a standing position. "Where?"

"We need to get you to the Mazikeen village. You are already starting through the change."

"I'm not changing, that was a little PMS moment."

"I'm not talking about what just happened. I'm talking about the change that all Mazikeen women must undergo to come into their power—the Kintala. You must be with a healer when that happens. I can't trust myself to help you."

"Right, the change you refuse to tell me about."

He ignored her and continued. "Soon, you will become weak and dizzy and it is best that you be with one of our healers when that happens. It makes the change easier. I have not been alone with a female during the change. And with you it is even more dangerous. I am not sure what I would do."

"What do you mean, what you would do? Like hurt me?"

He closed the small backpack and slung it over his head and onto his back. He then added a sweater and furred jacket she hadn't noticed before. He wedged them just below his neck, between the straps in the back. Then he found a stick—about two feet long. He unsheathed his knife and whittled one end to a very sharp point. He handed it to her. "I would never hurt you, Wynbune. But the pheromones are strong—even now. And if you begged me to be with you, I'm not sure I could resist— even with my duty clear, I am still a man."

She swallowed hard. What was he saying? That this Kintala thing would make her fall in love and want to have sex all day? Uh no. That wasn't gong to happen. She took the pointed stick from him. "And this is what I'm supposed to use to fight you off?"

He chuckled. "No, you would not be fighting me. You would be begging for me to touch you, to kiss you, to..."

Her breath caught in her throat. Not being around other

boys she wasn't sure if he was attracted to her or if this was some game all boys played to get you to have sex with them. She worried the bottom of her lip. He wasn't bad looking, and she did feel safe with him. Or at least she did before he started talking like this.

"You're pretty sure of yourself aren't you?" She pointed the stick at him. "Well you're not all that hot," she lied. "I've read books. I know what hot is and you are not that. So, just get it out of your head that anything is going to happen…ever."

Ohar laughed and shook his head. "I could take that from you with ease."

"Could not." She jabbed it in his direction and he easily ducked away.

She jabbed again, not really trying to hurt him and he grabbed it firmly with his hand and pulled her off balance. She fell toward him and he wrapped an arm around her, holding her up as she grabbed at his shirt and curled against his chest for balance. She breathed in his scent, a combination of musk and forest. Her senses came alive like an electric current was suddenly pulsing up and down every surface of her skin. Confused, she pushed away from him and dropped the stick beside her.

"Whoa! What was that?" She shook her hands in front of her, still feeling the current pulsing there.

He retrieved the stick and handed it back. "The stick is to fight off other things that we may encounter in our journey. As for me, I will hope that I have earned my status as a horned hunter and can keep you safe—even from me."

He took her face in his hands, and her heart seemed to stop as she looked into his eyes. The deep pools of blue mesmerized her. Her heart accelerated and she couldn't help but wet her lips as the excitement skittered down her spine in anticipation. Was he going to kiss her? She wanted him to. Oh god, she really wanted him to.

"I would prefer that you walk into the village on your own, Wynbune," he said, his voice almost a whisper. "However, I am prepared to carry you. If need be I will carry you even now."

She wasn't sure where her breath went, or why her heart seemed stopped in the moment. She struggled with her balance as the forest loam beneath her feet actually moved in a wave.

"Earthquake," Ohar shouted and pushed her to the ground, his arm breaking her fall and his body covering hers. He tucked her head into his chest. She struggled against him, suddenly afraid of her feelings. "No." He whispered in her ear. "Stay low until it passes. The forest will protect you. No harm will come to you."

She stopped moving and closed her eyes tight, unsure whether to be relieved or disappointed. She'd thought the sudden wave beneath her feet and the feeling of disorientation was the equivalent of romantic fireworks—proof that she and Ohar were meant to be together...as a couple. But an earthquake? Well, that kind of ruined the moment.

Though it was probably only twenty or thirty seconds, it felt like several minutes before Ohar rolled off her and stood, leaving her feeling even more off kilter. He once more offered his hand to help her up from the ground.

She accepted it, letting him pull her to a standing position. Not knowing what to say next, she instead purposefully brushed leaves and dirt from her garments.

Ohar cleared his throat. "You, uh, seemed to have grown significantly older."

She looked at her hands and groaned. Brown spots. "What color is my hair?"

"Dark brown, a little grey here and there, but not much."

"My mother," she said, deflated. "I guess, I couldn't hang on to me anymore."

"So you take on your mother's identity when you are frightened?"

"I...I guess so. At least that's what Dr. Frenelli always said." She searched for the stick he'd given her earlier. When she found it she stood and stiffened her spine, determined not to show any more fear. There would definitely be no romantic fireworks now. Let's face it, there is no way Ohar would want to kiss a fifty-five year old woman.

"Let's go—wherever it is we're going," she said. "Do you think the Mazikeen, or the healer can help me find who I really am, can help me stay with one identity?"

Ohar looked in her eyes, the pools of blue-grey seemed to be filled with understanding, and maybe just a little sadness. "The healer will help your body with the change, but only you can determine who you are—who you must be."

She turned away from his gaze, afraid he would see her true fear—that no amount of work on her part would ever help to reveal her true self. That maybe there really was no one inside —that she was destined to forever be someone else. She wiped at her eyes with the back of one hand. "My name is Camryn, not Wynbune. I ask you to remember that. That *is* a part of who I am."

He was silent, his eyes not on her but off to one side. Then he rolled his shoulders back and looked directly at her. "I apologize...Wyn...Camryn. I will try to call you by your chosen name."

She questioned for a moment what she was giving up with the other name. It was different. Like a fairytale name. No, Camryn was hers, only hers. This was a good start. The name

Camryn was the one thing she was sure of—the one constant throughout her life.

Camryn reached toward him, her fingers hesitating for a moment. Then she touched his chin and moved it back to center. She made full eye contact with him. "Good for remembering my name…Camryn." She smiled at Ohar and dropped her hand from his face. "Okay then, let's go. If this change thing is going to happen soon, and I'm going to be dizzy and weak and out of control, I want to get to wherever it is we're going."

"Good," he said with an acknowledging nod. He turned on his heel and led the way across the now dry meadow. "If we make good time, we may get to the village by midnight. If we can run part of the way—we may be even earlier."

STORM CLOUDS

*A*fter several miles of alternating running and walking, Ohar looked behind him more often, keeping an eye on the Chameleon. She seemed to be tripping over roots more and scraping her legs on sharp bushes. But she hadn't complained at all for the first two hours.

"Can we stop?" she asked.

He turned as she balanced herself against a tree trunk.

"I...I need to..."

Ohar reached out just in time to catch her as she passed out. He swore at his thoughtlessness, and carefully carried her to a patch of soft lichen and held her against him in one arm as he dropped his pack off the other arm. Still holding her, he withdrew the sweater and wrapped it like a pillow. He lowered her head to the pillow and covered her with his furred jacket, realizing she would cool quickly.

He swore again at himself. He knew she'd be getting weaker, yet he was so concentrated on moving quickly he hadn't paid enough attention. She'd seemed to be keeping up without a problem. He was pushing them so fast because he was determined not to be alone with her during the change. He knew her hormones would be raging and she would be willing to do all kinds of things. He didn't trust himself not to take advantage of her when that happened.

There was little question already that he was drawn to her in every way, no matter her outward look. But these feeling were purely hormonal—not love. Being in the presence of a Mazikeen woman during the change effected all males around her. That is why he had to get her to his tribe, to get her into the hands of a healer to take over.

Ohar still loved Lyra. He would never forget her, even if she'd chosen the void over staying. Though he could not give the Chameleon his heart, he would do his duty and take Camryn as his mate after the Kintala. He would do his best to make her happy and to help her save his people. That is, if she chose him. The choice had to be hers. He would have to be careful and not push her, not let her hormones dictate the pace —instead giving her heart time to determine what to do.

She'd changed significantly since they'd began their trek. It had not been long after they started running that Wynbune... no, Camryn ...had changed back to a more youthful girl. It was as if her body knew she had to transform to keep up. He wondered if this new image was someone she'd known, a composite, or maybe the true one she sought. Maybe the true Camryn emerged when her body was in tune and her mind unfocused on her identity. It was confusing for him, and he couldn't begin to imagine how awful it had been for her all this time, not knowing anything of the ways of the forest people.

He looked back at her in repose—so beautiful, so strong. If only she would embrace her calling, then the power would well in her quickly and she would know her true self, from the inside. The outside would then take care of itself. This new woman beside him was similar to the first one he'd met at the Starlight Center, but not the same. She appeared a little older and more confident than he remembered. Her dark hair had shortened, perhaps to keep her cool. It was still wavy—maybe more so now that it was short.

She stirred a little under his jacket. Then her eyes flew open and she threw the wrap away from her as she sat up. "What happened? Where are we?" She looked around, a wariness in her eyes.

"I was tired," Ohar said as he handed her an encu bar prepared by the healer a week ago. "You must have been as well, because you fell asleep as soon as we stopped."

She raised a brow and tilted her head to one side. "Really? I don't remember stopping. In fact, I don't remember..." She looked behind her at the sweater he had made into a pillow, then back at him. "I...did you...?" She picked up the jacket she had discarded. "I don't understand."

He reached for the jacket, and when she let go he slowly rolled it to put back in his pack. "Nothing to worry about," he said. "You were a little dizzy, and tired, and you needed a rest."

"I passed out, didn't I?" She started to stand, but wobbled and sat back down. "Oooo. I'm still dizzy."

Ohar pointed to the encu bar she still held in her hand. "Eat. Please. It will help. I promise." He took a bite from his own bar and chewed purposefully to show her it was okay. "They don't taste like much, but they are filled with energy."

Camryn tentatively bit off a small edge. Then she smiled and took a larger bite. "Mmmmmm. Tastes like chocolate. You really come prepared, don't you? Are you like a boy scout for the forest people?"

"Boy scout?" That wasn't a term he knew, and he thought he

knew most of the Agnoses words. He had prepared to integrate with them since he was twelve, often interacting at campgrounds with boys near his own age to make sure he could one day converse with them in case they needed to make a treaty. He shook his head. "What is a boy scout?"

She laughed as if he were teasing. When he said nothing, she scrunched her brow. "You really don't know?"

He shook his head, and took another bite of his encu bar.

"It's a person who's taught how to do stuff in the wilderness. They go camping and hiking, and tie knots, and one of their mottos is always be prepared." She took another bite of the encu bar. "Oh, and they help old ladies across the street and stuff like that. And they're honest and trustworthy. Well, you get the picture."

He was still confused. Most of what she said was true, except for the helping old ladies across the street part. There were not roads in most of the People's forests—though Agnoses had tried to make them in some parts of the forests, pushing at the barrier between the Forest People and their world. And the Mazikeen grandmothers did not need help. They were strong on their own. In fact, the power of the Mazikeen grandmothers was not to be questioned.

"We do not have this term, boy scout," he said. "But many of the things you described are a part of the lessons of life. The People live always in the forest. We know how to live without shelter, how to gather the food needed to maintain these bodies, and how to work together with other forest peoples to sustain the earth. You have this same calling, Camryn. You can do all these things. You are one of us. You are the chosen one— the Chameleon."

She shook her head. "I don't think so. I don't know half the things you've described. I love the forest. I've always felt protected—special—among the trees. But I don't understand them. I'm sure if my biological parents came from your people then my parents would have told me."

Ohar sighed. He didn't know why he kept trying to tell her of her calling. The old ones had warned him that she wouldn't believe. She would have to come into her belief after the change, after it was irrefutable that she and the forest were one. The old ones kept saying: "Patience, Ohar," as if he had the ability to be patient. They'd promised she would believe in time —in time to fight the Abaddon. He hoped so, because at this pace he wasn't sure she'd ever get there. Was it possible that with her adoptive parent's death, the prophecy could not be fulfilled? Was it possible that this one accident had doomed them all?

The scryers had no advance warning of the accident. All the people had depended on her adoptive mother to be there for the Chameleon. The woman who had cared for Camryn had been one part Mazikeen and one part Agnoses. She had chosen to marry an Agnoses man, even knowing they could never have children together. But she'd never forgotten her loyalty to the People. That was why she'd been the perfect choice. It seemed the old ones didn't know everything, after all. But he had no choice but to trust and to carry on, hoping that Camryn made the right choices in the end.

"Wow. Looks like storm clouds are crowding your brain." Camryn interrupted his melancholy thoughts.

"Sorry," he said. "I was gathering wool as the Agnoses say."

"You've used that term several times now. What does that mean? Agnoses?"

"It means the ones who do not see...do not believe what their own experience dictates."

"Oh, you mean agnostic. Like people who don't believe in God but don't disbelieve in God."

"That is close," he said. "It is the belief that all of the forest people know to be true…the interconnectedness of all things. That we are an integral part of that connection, but no more or less important than anything else. You know it Camryn, though you have not put a name to it. That is why you feel the protection of the forest even though you have not grown up with us. There are some in the Agnoses world who also feel it, truly feel it in their very being. Some of them choose to leave the Agnoses world and when they go into the forest, the forest chooses who will be accepted. Those who are accepted join us. Others try but their mind does not allow them to make the transition fully. They become our ambassadors on the outside. They do good work."

"How can you be so sure?" she asked. "How can you be so sure I feel it, that I am one of the forest people?"

He took both her hands in his and bowed his head. "Close your eyes as I hold your hands."

She giggled, but did not struggle or take her hands away. He watched her until her eyes closed.

"Open your mind to the forest, just as you did last night when you followed the lights."

He felt her hesitation, her fear of the unknown, but after only a few moments she did begin to let go—first only a little and then more and more. He sent his essence into the forest floor and called the lichen to send its power—to reach for that part of her that had opened to the forest. When he found that small part of her essence he latched on. She gasped and started to withdraw but he held tight until she allowed herself to join with him and the forest again. Then his mind reached out to the trees around him and asked for their blessing. Together they linked with the deer and the fox, with the bear and the snake, with the wild huckleberries and the rhododendron. They linked with the lichen network that infused the forest.

Together, they breathed as one, feeling each breath enter and leave as if they were the lungs of the forest. Together, as one, the blood pulsed through their veins with the same life-giving oxygen that pulsed through the trees, the animals of the forest, the ferns of the canyons. The same oxygen that brings the whales to the surface of the sea.

~

CAMRYN WRAPPED herself in Ohar's arms and pulled his mouth toward hers. Their kiss reflected the oneness of all things—the love of the universe reflected through them. Kiss? She pushed against his chest, confused. But he held her tight.

"Oh my god. Oh my god. Oh my god!" The feelings that overcame her, the experience of the interconnectedness of all things. She couldn't believe it. It was too weird...too amazing...too...

"Trust what you experienced," he said. "The prophecy is true. It is only together that we will defeat the Abaddon." He slowly released her.

The coolness of the forest surrounded her once more. The growing darkness was strange after feeling so much light and warmth. A foggy mist drifted toward them, and on the edges she heard a deep laughter.

Ohar pushed her behind him and withdrew the knife from his scabbard, holding it in front of him. "Show yourself Boha'a thief. I know it's you."

Out of the mist stepped a man who was near Ohar's age but at least a foot taller and many pounds heavier. A five o'clock shadow of a beard made her wonder if he might be older or just unkept. The hair on his head was so thick Camryn was unsure if it might have a life of its own. He leaned nonchalant against the tree beside him, the neck of his shirt open, and watched her. Large silver hoops in his ears and rings on his fingers reflected a light through the mist.

"Step no further toward us," Ohar said. "State your business and be gone."

The man laughed again. "So this is the Chameleon? Come out child, you have nothing to fear from me."

"Don't listen," Ohar said, keeping her behind him. "He is a Boha'a thief. He cares for nothing but riches and pleasure. He would kidnap you for his own ends."

"He tells the truth," the man said, unmoving from his place. "I am a thief. And I would never turn away from pleasure when it is presented. But I never lie. I am Dagger, and I am at your service Wynbune."

Camryn did not move from behind Ohar. How is it everyone knew this Wynbune name and seemed to know everything about her when she barely knew herself?

"Has Ohar told you about your father?" The man said.

Camryn peered around Ohar's back. "What about my father?"

"Don't listen," Ohar said. "He knows nothing."

Dagger stepped forward. He was slow, but not at all wary. Suddenly, Ohar's knife was in Dagger's hand and Ohar was no longer in front of her.

"That was uncalled for, Dagger, even for you," Ohar mumbled from about twenty feet away.

Dagger threw the knife away from him, but looked straight at Camryn as he spoke. "You know better than to threaten me. The Boha'a are faster, smarter, stronger than any Mazikeen."

His eyes, Camryn had never seen such eyes. One was cerulean blue, with flecks of green. It was as if she could see the ocean in them. The other was gold, like the sun, but with a dark rim of black around the edge. Dagger's eyes glowed in his darkened face, uneven, and strange. They didn't seem human. She couldn't stop looking at them, and there was no doubt he was staring at her. Camryn's heart fumbled a beat and, in that pause, a feeling of gloomy darkness slid like a shadow over her. It vanished in an instant, but she was still staring at him. His smile wasn't friendly. It was a smile that spelled trouble. With a promise.

"Ah. You are not as young as I thought. Sixteen? Seventeen?" Dagger reached to grasp her hand in his, but Camryn stepped back.

"Sixteen, as if it's any of your business," she said.

Dagger laughed, his head thrown back and his beard shaking with mirth. "So young and feisty. You already bring me pleasure, Wynbune."

Ohar scrambled back to her side. "Back away," he ordered Dagger. "She is going through the Kintala, you cannot be near."

Dagger's gaze traveled the length of her body and smiled. "Better for me to be near than you, Mazikeen. I will know what to do with her as her hormones run away. All you would do is berate yourself for your desire."

Camryn reached up and slapped him across one cheek. "Don't talk as if I'm not here and have no choice."

Dagger rubbed at the redness in his cheek but he stood his ground. "I am glad to see you have a spine. That bodes well for your future." He lifted his chin. "Your choice is the Mazikeen or the Boha'a. I will escort you to the Boha'a if you wish."

"I'm not going anywhere with you. I know nothing about you. Ohar has been kind. He has protected me. He has never attacked me—never made untoward advances. He is nothing like you."

Dagger chuckled. "We are, indeed, nothing alike." He held his arms out to the side. "I am exactly what you see, nothing more. You will always know where you stand. You may not like what I say or what I do, but I will hold no secrets from you." He paused and pointed to Ohar. "Unlike the Mazikeen, who are filled with secrets. Did you know the Mazikeen already have you mated with Ohar?"

Ohar sputtered beside her. "That's not—

"At least I am honest about what I want," Dagger continued. He wrapped a piece of her hair around his finger. "I find you attractive. I will take advantage of you during the Kintala if you do not fight me off. I will not hide that. But I will not force anything on you, and when you beg me to be with you I will be there. I will not walk away."

Camryn could barely catch her breath. This wasn't right. He shouldn't talk like this—like he would be her lover. She'd never had a lover. She'd thought of it, of course, but this was too fast. This was too confusing. Her breath came faster and faster, her pulse raged out of control. She could no longer focus on Dagger's face or his words.

He reached for her as she became dizzy. The mist welled up around her. She gasped as he pulled her closer and she went under. The darkness of a stormy night arose in her vision. She again felt connected to the forest, but this time connected to the dark lichen that choked the last life out of dying trees. Connected to raging storms and the frightening power of light-ning. She shivered as a cold, damp breeze whipped around them.

Dagger's voice spoke in her ear as he held her tight. "I will not touch you and make you feel safe and warm. I am not of the light. The Boha'a are in the shadows. Our needs are immediate. Our desires are known to all. There is no subterfuge. I will connect you with the dark and give you a choice."

She awoke once again on the ground. Dagger pulled her to a sitting position and she shivered with cold.

"Ohar is holding secrets. You should ask about them before making a choice. He is not what he seems."

Camryn looked up to see Ohar kneeling in front of her. "What secrets are you holding from me?"

Ohar touched her and she again felt the warmth of the forest through him. Unlike her experience with Dagger, she felt safe, protected. She struggled to separate that feeling from what was happening. She removed his hand from her arm and immediately felt the cold fog surrounding them.

"What are you withholding from me?" she repeated.

Ohar remained silent.

Dagger stood and crossed his arms across his chest. "For one, your father is held prisoner by the Mazikeen."

She scrambled back to stand and stepped away from Ohar. "Is it true? Your people are holding my father? My biological father?"

She saw the swallow in Ohar's throat. He stood and looked out to the horizon. "It is true that we hold him. He broke a sacred law and for that he has been imprisoned."

"And you were going to tell me this when?"

Dagger reached for her and she slapped his hand away. "Don't touch me. I don't know you and I don't trust you either."

"But you trust Ohar?" he asked. "You know what sacred law your father broke? He fell in love with your mother, a Mazikeen. That's all."

Ohar stiffened beside her, his lips clamped shut as if he couldn't trust himself not to speak.

Dagger laughed. "What a web of deceit the Mazikeen weave. All that warmth and light comes at a cost. Control of everyone and everything. Your father is Quatcho and your mother is Mazikeen. The two groups have never been allowed together because the Quatcho must birth their babies in nature, whereas the Mazikeen bring forth children only with magic."

"There is good reason for the stricture," Ohar said, his voice controlled. His words slowly articulated. "And your mother paid with her life to love your father."

Camryn gasped. "You mean you killed her? You killed her for falling in love with someone from a different place?"

"No!" Ohar grabbed her by both shoulders. "We would never kill one of our own. We are not murderers. It was your father who killed her."

"Not true," Dagger interrupted, removing Ohar's hands from her shoulders.

Camryn stepped away. She was getting tired of being between them, tired of feeling warm one moment and cold the next.

Ohar locked his jaw and stared down Dagger. "It is true. It is because he forced himself on her, impregnated her, then she died."

"There was no forcing involved," Dagger said. "They loved each other."

"He impregnated her. She died." Ohar insisted.

"He made love to her. She got pregnant. She died in childbirth. She knew the risks and she accepted them." Dagger looked directly at Camryn. "If she hadn't you would not be here today. Out of that love, came the first Chameleon in a millennium. You."

Camryn could barely take it in. She'd been told her mother died in childbirth. She'd been told her father was unable to take care of her. But she didn't know the circumstances. Now, she was no longer sure what she should do—who she should trust.

She looked at Ohar. "Has my father been imprisoned all this time? Ever since my birth?"

"No, not that long," Ohar said.

Dagger chuckled. "Not for lack of trying. They just couldn't find him for the first ten years."

"So for six years he's been in prison?" Camryn asked. "For falling in love?"

"He makes it out to be worse than it is. When I get you back to the village, you will understand. The grandmothers will explain. It will make sense. I know it sounds bad right now, but you have to trust me, Camryn." Ohar took her hand. "Let's go now. I can see you are still weak. We cannot wait much longer."

"That's true," Dagger said. "You don't want to wait much longer. You need a healer to help you through the Kintala. The question is if the Mazikeen should be the ones to help you."

Ohar looked at her again. "You do not want to live with the Boha'a. They are thieves. They have no morals."

Dagger laughed again. "This coming from a man who imprisons your father for the crime of love. A man who has been instructed to bring you back to his people so they can make sure you mate. A man who knows that his touch brings you warmth and a feeling of safety. But ask yourself, is it real?" He pointed an accusing finger at Ohar. "This is a man who has not told you all of the truth, and has not given you a choice. He controls your every move. When he touches you, your changes stop. Right?"

Camryn looked at Ohar and raised a brow. How did Dagger know how Ohar affected her?

"Why do you trust Ohar?" Dagger demanded. "How do you know he is not taking you to prison as well?"

She hadn't really thought about why she trusted Ohar. In fact, she wasn't sure about anything anymore.

"I'm not taking you to prison," Ohar said. "He's trying to trick you. He only wants you for his own needs."

"No doubt," Dagger said. "But I won't lie to you about it. I won't try to make you into someone you are not. I won't try to make you save my people at a cost to all other species. If you come with me, you can be whoever you want to be. I will give you choice."

"Don't listen to him," Ohar said. "He is with the shadows. You are the Chameleon. You are light. You are the chosen one of the Mazikeen."

Camryn rubbed her temples. Her head hurt and she wasn't sure what to believe. "What does that mean anyway? The chosen one. What is it I'm supposed to do?"

"To fight the Abbadon, to restore the forest lichen to its true form, to stop the Agnoses."

"In short," Dagger interrupted, "to save the Mazikeen world." Then he suddenly pushed Ohar away, grabbed Camryn and held her tight against him.

"No!" She fought him, wriggling in his embrace with what little strength she had. But the more she fought, the weaker she became. Why was it she was so weak? When she entered the forest only yesterday, she'd been strong and sure.

The mist closed around them and the cold enveloped her once again. She could no longer see anything except Dagger's chest. Then the ground disappeared beneath her feet. The trees swirled around her. The wind blew her hair behind her and she shivered. Dagger pulled his cloak around her and she burrowed her face into his embrace. She barely heard Ohar's wail wafting in the breeze and then there was nothing.

KINTALA

The swirling wind and rain lifted as suddenly as it began and Camryn felt the ground steady her balance. She quickly backed away from Dagger.

"How dare you!"

He shrugged his shoulders. "You will thank me in the end. Trust me."

"Trust you?" Her voice rose to a shriek? "Trust you? Are you out of your mind?" She pointed her index finger at him, her entire body shaking with anger. "I did not give you permission to take me. I did not want to go with you. I do not believe anything you've said. And, I do not want to be here. Take me back this instant!"

Dagger threw back his head and laughed so hard his entire body shook. "You think all you have to do is demand and I will obey? The Boha'a take what they want and do not need permission. When…if…I determine it is appropriate to take you back I will."

"I can't believe...I can't...Why you..." Camryn sputtered, unable to put any words to her anger.

"Noooooooooooo!" The pain hit her forehead first, then traveled down her neck. A thousand small sticks beat its way down her spine, doubling her over. She hadn't felt this bad during the change since entering the forest. What was wrong?

I will not turn into him. I will not turn into him. I will not. I will not. I will not! Her skin stretched and bones creaked with such pain she fell to her knees as her limbs expanded and her torso grew taller. She screamed and fell onto her back, barely able to breathe as a vice crushed her center from shoulder to pelvis. Her breasts disappeared and the bones in her chest expanded to match the broad barrel of Dagger's chest. Tears streamed from her eyes, settling in the heavy beard she now wore.

Breathe. Just breathe. Camryn took a careful breath in and held it, even with the feeling of hammers still beating against her ribs. Squeezing her eyes closed, she let the breath out slowly, and then counted. *One. Breathe in. Breathe out. Two. Breathe in. Breathe out. Three.*

"It's true," a feminine voice whispered. "She looks just like Dagger."

"It's the Chameleon," another said, a younger voice.

"Back away. Give her space." She recognized Dagger's voice. For once he wasn't mocking her.

"Let me in. Let me in." An older voice, ragged, scratchy. "Leave. All of you."

Feet shuffled away and Camryn breathed again. *Fourteen. Breathe in. Breathe out. Fifteen. Breathe in. Breathe out. Sixteen.*

"You too, Dagger," the scratchy voice demanded. "Out. You are the last person who should be here. You will draw on her hormones. Go! Go!"

Grumbled words she couldn't make out, then heavy, sure steps receded.

After several minutes, Camryn thought she must finally be alone. She opened her eyes only a little—just enough to peer beneath her lashes and take in her immediate surroundings.

"The beard is not the best look for you, dear."

The older, ragged voice was still here.

"You can open your eyes. I'm the only one here now. But, if we don't get moving we will both have visitors you won't like." The older woman paused, then placed a gnarled hand under her elbow. "Come on now. Sit up. If you are the image of Dagger, I have to believe you also have his strength."

Camryn shot to her feet and took inventory. *Damn. Damn. Damn.* She was still a man, and not a man she admired. She stared at the hunched old woman now standing in front of her. No, turning into her was not going to be helpful. She closed her eyes and concentrated. Taking deep breaths she repeated the one image she owned, the one she had built at Starlight Center. *Chestnut hair, curly, waist length. Blue eyes. Tan skin. No wrinkles. Five feet, five inches tall, one hundred twenty pounds.* The tingles started and she sucked in a breath, determined not to scream out this time. *Chestnut hair, curly, waist length. Blue eyes...* Camryn pitched forward. The change was happening fast this time. She swallowed and wrapped her arms around her stomach. *Five feet, five inches tall, one hundred twenty pounds. Chestnut hair, curly...*

"Is the pain worse than before?" the woman asked. "It's the Kintala. Your hormones are flooding your system. It makes each change harder, more painful. You must be taken to the Alder. You must be put to sleep."

Camryn grunted and moaned as she curled into a fetal position. Her arms and legs retracted. Her chest compressed and her breath rushed from her lungs. Breasts sprouted where a mat of manly hair had been only minutes before. She gritted her teeth. Just a little longer. *Tan skin. Blue eyes...* All at once the pain disappeared. She slowly straightened and stood, her hand scrubbing at the dried tears staining her cheeks.

"Beautiful." The old woman barely whispered the compliment. "Congratulations, Wynbune. You are learning control."

Camryn took inventory. She fingered her hair, pulling it forward within her sight. Yes! It was long again. It was curly. She was female. She'd returned. She'd made a choice and returned to the identity she'd chosen. She took in a deep breath and exhaled, lifting her chin slightly. She held her hand out to the woman. "My name is Camryn. And you are?"

Two gnarled hands, with raised pulsing green spots, enveloped hers. "I am called Abrani Daj, the mother healer for the Boha'a."

A soothing mist traveled from Abrani's hand and up Camryn's arm. It swirled about her head. Camryn closed her eyes as it cloaked her entire body. This was not the stormy cold, nor the powerful lightning she had experienced with Dagger. Instead, Abrani's touch offered a deep well full of cold, sweet and refreshing water to slake her thirst.

Abrani fingered the dreamcatcher Camryn still wore around her neck. "This was Fia's."

"Fia?"

"Your birth mother." Abrani tapped the center of the dreamcatcher. "Your mother had powerful magic, filled with light. She provided a protection spell here." Abrani closed her eyes and swayed. "Yes...and focus magic. This is good. Very good. It will help you during the Kintala."

"How? How will it help me? What happens in the Kintala? What am I supposed to do?"

Abrani tugged at Camryn's arm. "We must move you to the Matriarch Alder." She pointed to a clearing in the forest, where a substantial tree grew among the redwoods. Among the lowest branches was some type of platform with a canvas shade over the top, similar to the treehouse her father had built when she was young. She could barely make out the edges of what appeared to be bedding on a raised pallet.

"That is where you will be protected. That is where you can endure the Kintala in peace." Abrani grabbed her hand and roughly towed her toward the tree.

Camryn dug in her feet and pulled back. "Wait. Tell me about the Kintala. Tell me what will happen."

"No time. No time. The change is coming fast now." Abrani again pulled her toward the tree, this time with even more force.

At the base of the alder, Camryn studied the perch above her. The lowest branch was a good twelve feet or more above the ground. "Um. I'm not sure that's such a great idea. How do I get up there? What if I need to come down, to…you know…"

"That is not a worry," Abrani said. "The tree will harbor you, meet all your needs. Now hurry." She tugged again and positioned Camryn with her back to the large red alder. She held her hand to Camryn's stomach as she began a singing chant. "Alder mother shield this child. Shield this child. Shield this child."

Camryn stepped away. "Wait! Ohar said the Boha'a are dark and the Mazikeen are light. I don't want to be cold and dark."

Abrani pushed her back. "There is no time. You will be what you will be, both light and dark. It is written."

Camryn pushed back. "Wait. Just wait a minute. I'm not doing anything until I understand what is going on here. You seem like a nice enough person, but things have not been exactly normal for me lately."

"No time. I cannot protect you. Only the lichen can protect you. Quick." Abrani pushed at her again, this time pinning her to the tree with a strength Camryn did not think she had. "Hold. Shield. Hold. Shield. " Abrani commanded, but Camryn could see no one to obey. Abrani sang her chant again. "Alder mother shield this child of Mazikeen and Quatcho, shield her from the Abaddon."

Heavy green lichen pressed on Camryn's shoulders. She tried to duck, but more lichen wrapped around her middle, binding her to the tree. Camryn cried out in alarm.

Abrani's words were muffled now. "The confidence of a fox. The bravery of an owl. The spirit of the wolf. Protect her. Protect her."

The lichen reached Camryn's neck and crawled up her face, obscuring her vision. It pulsed light and dark as she struggled against its embrace.

"Shield the here, the now, the past, the future. Shield the astral self from intrusion from other realms." Abrani pushed against the lichen, which now strangled Camryn's chest. "Go! Go! Go!"

The tree shook. The lichen pulsed faster. A cold wind cycled, lifting the strands of Camryn's hair, giving each piece a life of its own. The air smelled sharp as new-cut wood, slicing low and sly around the exposed roots at her feet. Lithe brown arms of wood encircled her like a legion of snakes. Hissing air. Compressing air. Stealing air.

Vfffff. She was sucked into the tree, traveling its capillaries as if in a pneumatic tube. She struggled for breath. Frost pierced through her ribs and crept toward her heart, filling the hollow places between pulses of blood.

She opened her mouth to scream, but lichen filled it, paralyzing her.

The tree bound her in lichen then threw her out onto the pallet bed with a hard thud.

Her breath stilled.

Her heart stopped.

Her mind silenced.

White wings beat at her unconscious and called her name. A winged dragon rose from a frigid mountaintop and soared over snow plains and caves, far from the warming rays of the sun. *Food. Food.* Impatient. The white dragon swept toward her, talons extended. *Food. Food.*

The Alder cried out. *Shield! Shield!* Lights pulsed in her lichen cocoon and warmed Camryn's bed. Her heart jumped. Her breath returned. The dragon passed over.

Peace. The Alder crooned.

She slept.

A constant chattering intruded. On the ground, a large, green-scaled bird destroyed the understory of ferns. It tore insects from their nests. It threw mice against the tree and then chomped them in half. It squawked and rose above her bed shaking larger prey, the blood pelting her forehead as the bird consumed it. It dove and returned again and again, screeching incessantly—screaming misery, misfortune, woe, despair.

Camryn wept.

Out of the clouds, an alien canine beast peered down at her. *Windigo.* The word appeared in her thoughts as the beast morphed into the image of Dagger. A Dagger who craved human flesh. He plunged from the sky into a camp of humans on the outskirts of the forest. As they ran for cover, Dagger caught a young woman in his embrace and devoured her as she screamed. Blood filled his mouth and he reared back his head in violent triumph and called out her name, drawing out the sound as a lover would lure in his mate. *Camryn. Camryn.*

She cowered in fear, not sure if she was dreaming or awake to witness the atrocity. She prayed for release. She sought an end, even death.

Peace, the Alder crooned.

A blanket of warmth covered her. She calmed and inhaled the smell of lilacs. Glorious sunlight filled the valley with purple fire. A ghostly Ohar hovered above her. Behind him, clouds rolled, sinking, rising, like low swells of a gold and purple sea. His smile invited her confidence. His eyes glowed with desire. He slowly moved a plain wooden staff along her body, hovering only inches above it.

"Lyra," he called. "Lyra."

She saw herself changing into someone else, even though she had never met this girl. Her hair turned the color of sunshine and grew to her waist. Her limbs lengthened another two inches and she slimmed to be at least twenty pounds lighter. Whenever she turned, rays of light radiated from her.

"It is you," Ohar said. "I have missed you so much." He moved the staff along her body again. Wherever it lingered, she warmed and passion stirred. Her mouth opened for his kiss. Her breasts arched for his touch. Her center writhed with want. Her mind lashed out in denial, but her body—not her body, the body of this person called Lyra—contradicted her command. She moaned as her hormones awakened and her body arched with need toward the angelic Ohar.

"Stop! Camryn. Wake." A tongue laved her cheek. "Stop! Camryn. Wake." A furry paw rested on her neck. "Protect! Shield! Shield!" A furry head bumped against her side. "Camryn Wake…Wake. Now."

KOŠKA

*H*er body settled again upon the pallet and the wanton heat diffused, the sun gently grazing Camryn's eyelids in a final kiss. She carefully turned her head to one side, away from the light. A large cat lounged next to her, nodded, then stretched and stood. Before her eyes, the cat morphed into a young girl of about twelve. With her back to Camryn, her gold-flecked, brown and black hair was the same color as the cat's fur. It hung in thick, straight locks almost to her knees, covering her nakedness. The girl reached into a satchel, secreted in a nook of the tree, and pulled on a cerulean shift before turning around.

"I am Koška," she said, pushing her thick hair behind her shoulders.

Camryn tried to sit, but couldn't find the strength to move. She panted breaths and her heart raced in panic. Her memory of Ohar's searing heat paralyzed her.

Koška gracefully settled at Camryn's side and positioned both palms against her forehead. It was as if a cool washcloth had been placed across her fevered brow. The heat slowly dissipated, beginning with her head and then traveling down her neck and chest, until it finally extended to her limbs.

"Relax. It is part of the Kintala. It will pass in a couple of days."

Koška lifted Camryn's head and braced her back with her other hand to help her sit up.

Camryn worked to catch her breath. Her chest heaved, as if she were climbing with a sixty-pound pack. "Thank… you," she barely managed the words.

Koška offered her a piece of lichen dripping with water. "Drink. It will restore you."

Camryn recoiled. "No." Camryn's voice scraped out. "No more lichen."

"Please," Koška implored. "You don't need to eat, just let the water drip into your throat. The lichen is part of your DNA now. You must ingest it regularly to maintain your powers."

Reluctant, Camryn tilted back her head and opened her mouth. Koška squeezed the lichen's water onto Camryn's tongue. Each swallow lessened the heaviness. Each swallow gave her more strength.

"How long?" She asked. "How long have I been here?"

"I'm not sure," Koška said. "I was called by your screams. Your fear. I've only been here a few hours, but given your state I would think four or five days have passed."

Camryn closed her eyes. Days. What else did she experience that she didn't even remember?

Koška sat back on her haunches. "Who was it you saw? What made you afraid?"

Camryn shook her head, unsure if she wanted to recall any of her dreams.

"It was my step-brother," Koška confirmed at the same time it came back to Camryn. "Whatever you saw is not true."

Camryn winced at the memory of being devoured by Dagger. Was it a warning? A sign? It was Dagger who had kidnapped her, stolen her from Ohar. He readily admitted to not having a conscience, to serving his own pleasure.

Koška stood and paced. "It is not truth," she repeated. "The visions during the Kintala are a reflection of your hormones, your fears, your hopes. It is your spirit searching for identity, searching for connection."

"And Ohar?" Camryn asked. Her hands automatically covered her chest as if even thinking about the dream would make her want him again.

"Was it sexual?"

Camryn nodded, unwilling to describe any of it.

"Did you smell lilacs?"

Again Camryn nodded. "He called me Lyra, and I changed to look like someone I've never met before. How can that be? How can I become someone I've never seen?"

"Long blonde hair that streams out like sunshine?" Koška asked.

"Yes! How did you know?"

"Damn him!" Koška pounded a fist into a low tree branch. "Lyra is his soulmate, who has gone to the void." Koška made a sign in the air that that looked like a circle with a line through it —like the coda in music. "May the lichen bless her." She paused and looked to the sky.

"Soulmate? But why? How? What does it have to do with me?"

"The Mazikeen Queen, Ohar's mother, is determined that he will marry you. He cannot love you because he has given his heart to Lyra, even though she is no longer of this world.

Because he is to be bound to you, he used the lilac wand to enhance sexual pleasure, and in that enhancement you are connected to his thoughts—which would be of Lyra."

Camryn could barely take in what Koška said. This world was not any safer than Starlight Center if magic could be used against her. "Do I have no recourse? This is not acceptable. First, I don't intend to be anyone's mate. Second, I have a hard enough time tracking my own changes without someone else forcing me to do it. I thought Ohar was helping me. I thought he actually cared how difficult it was for me." She tried to rise, but her legs would not move. It was as if they had no muscle.

"Easy." Koška stroked her arm. "This is your first time through the lichen. Most of us grow up with it and then when the Kintala occurs it is not so devastating. You need to rest."

"How can I rest when it seems I have no control over what is happening to me? Must I forego sleep until this is over?"

"I will look into this. The Mazikeen have promised they would not use their magic on anyone undergoing the Kintala. They are not allowed to bind anyone for marriage without choice. They have agreed not to do this. Oooooo. If I confirm it was him, I will—"

"Wait. Are you saying the dream with Dagger is false, but the…the sexual feelings with Ohar were true? He was…was using me?"

"I'm not sure, but it is possible." Koška said. "There are cases where the Mazikeen have penetrated the Alder's protection in the astral plane—particularly when they are more than two years past Kintu—the male change. Unlike the Boha'a, who have no time limits, the Mazikeen males must find a mate within five years of their Kintu onset or all power will be relinquished."

Camryn jumped up. "Well, that son of a ….I'm going to kill

him. So much for being bound by duty to be fair. That—ohhh." She grasped a branch and leaned. Her head swam with dizziness.

Koška steadied her and lowered her back to the pallet. "Careful, your mind is ahead of your body strength."

Camryn stilled.

"Perhaps I spoke too quickly about Ohar's intentions." Koška said. "Though it is likely him, there may be another explanation for what you experienced. There are dark forces, like his mother who has suffered the mutation, who would think nothing of taking advantage of you. She would stop at nothing to make sure you are bound. There are also those who come on the wings of thunder dragons and cast illusions to confuse and betray. They take pleasure in pain. I woke you before you could go too far. We don't know the full intent. It may have been someone else wanting you to believe it was him."

Camryn's heart stumbled a beat as she thought of other horrifying possibilities. The white wings of a dragon was her first memory, though no one flew with the dragon. Is it possible the person was hidden? She searched her dream.

Blood. Violence. Hunger.

She shook from the memory. "Like Dagger?" She asked. "Would he be able to do this?"

Koška worried her bottom lip. "I'm not sure." Her brows furrowed as she paused. Then she shook her head. "No. I can't believe Dagger would do this. I don't believe he would get pleasure from forcing you against your will."

Camryn wasn't so sure. Dagger was dangerous and she wouldn't put anything past him. "Are you sure? Absolutely positive he wouldn't…couldn't…do this?"

Koška took in a deep breath and turned away to look

through the tree canopy toward the Boha'a camp. She stared for what seemed like several minutes. "I'm…No. I can't be positive. The Dagger I knew…before my Kintala…would not have done this." She wrapped her arms around her middle and stilled again. "I don't really know." Barely above a whisper, her voice trembled. "I don't know how much he has changed in the last three years. I don't want to believe…I…" She turned back to Camryn. "I'm sorry."

"You have gone through the Kintala? You seem young, much younger than me."

Koška tilted her head forward and her long hair obscured her face. "I am thirteen in solar years, but my experiences are of a grown woman. My father is Boha'a, but my mother is a Fae cat-shifter, part of an outcast clan of the Mazikeen. Cat shifters mature early, we age twice as fast as Boha'as. The Kintala begins at eight solar years, but that is sixteen to a cat-shifter. Though I am thirteen solar years, and my human body looks like a young girl, my cat body and mind are twenty-six. Much to the chagrin of my step-brother."

"Dagger is your step-brother?" Camryn paused as she took in the statement. Could she trust Koška to tell the truth? Or would she be bound to protect her stepbrother? Koška seemed kind. Unlike Dagger. But every step Camryn took in this world had reinforced that all motives were suspect.

"And Dagger, how old is he?" Camryn asked. In spite of being afraid him, she also felt an attraction to him. But it wasn't like her attraction to Ohar. Ohar radiated kindness and light and warmth. Except in the dream. She shivered again at what had almost happened. What she had wanted to do.

Dagger was the opposite. Cold. Powerful. Dangerous. Mostly dangerous. Yet, she felt pulled to him. What was wrong with her? Did the Kintala make her want every man she met?

She could understand why she might like Ohar. But Dagger? It was clear she should feel nothing toward him. He'd never been kind. He'd given her no reason at all to care about him.

Koška laughed and placed her hands on her hips. "I see Dagger has been his usual stupid-ass self."

Camryn stared at Koška. "Are you reading my mind?"

"No. I can't read minds, but I can hear feelings. And yours are shouting at me. Believe me, you are not the first female to be conflicted about my stepbrother. He's had that effect on girls since he was twelve.

"Dagger is incorrigible. His solar age is seventeen and he has more than his required hormones. Boha'a men physically mature earlier than Mazikeen or any other, except Quatcho. Their mind on the other hand…Dagger can be strong and heroic when disaster is at hand, but most of the time he acts like a five-year-old, thinking only of himself and what he wants."

"So, you don't get along?"

"We love each other, but we haven't spoken in three years." Koška looked away. "Not since he realized what the sex life of a young cat is like. I can't stop being who I am until I find my mate. No matter how many times he commands otherwise." She shrugged her shoulders and rolled her head, stretching her neck, then turned back to Camryn. "He's not mad at me. Or so he says. He's mad at my mother for being Mazikeen, and particularly for being a cat-shifter. He's mad at my father, his father too, for choosing to be with a Mazikeen woman in any form. Of course, he believes my mother lured him to her. Which is crap. He sees the world through one lens, and when reality doesn't match up he simply refuses to accept it."

Camryn closed her eyes. She was so tired.

Koška kneeled beside her and patted her hand. "I'm sorry. I didn't mean to go on about Dagger. You are exhausted. The

Kintala does that." She pointed toward something hanging from the tree.

"Did you bring that?"

Camryn looked at the woven circle with feathers sticking out the sides. Her dreamcatcher! How did it get up here? She didn't remember taking it off. Who removed it? Who tied it to the tree?

"Is it yours?" Koška asked again.

Camryn nodded. "Yes, it is all I have left of my mother."

"That explains it. Fia had great magic. That is how I could hear your call, even though I was far away."

"The only mother I knew was named Bliant." Camryn swallowed hard. It had been a long time since she thought of her adopted mother. The drugs at Starlight Center had kept much of her grief at bay.

Koška lightly touched her arm. "And she was a great woman also. Your mother—I mean your birth mother—chose Bliant while she was pregnant with you. She knew she would die and she did not want to entrust you with the same people who had banished her and your father. She asked Bliant to raise you and when it was time for the Kintala to make sure you had a good teacher. Your mother was Mazikeen."

Camryn's eyes widened. "Like Ohar?"

Koška nodded. "You didn't know?"

"I only knew my biological parents died when I was a baby. I never knew their names. Bliant is…was… my adopted mother. She is the one who gave me the dreamcatcher."

"Then Fia must have made sure it was with you when you went to Bliant. Anyway, it can help you with the Kintala."

"How?"

"So far you have been dreaming. Next you will be tested. The dreamcatcher can help you to focus your powers. These tests are serious. Some have been known to die during the test. Always remember, you must fight! If you do not fight, you will die."

Camryn held up her hand in a stop motion. "Whoa. Whoa. Whoaaaaaa. What powers?"

"Your magic."

"But I don't have any magic. My shtick is this chameleon thing...you know the one I can't seem to control."

Koška laughed. "It's good to have a sense of humor, but this is serious, Camryn. You must have control of calling and manipulating the elements. In the void, you will be challenged as never before. If you don't call them to help you, you will fail."

Camryn suddenly felt ill. She wrapped her arms around her stomach and moaned. "Its too much. I don't understand anything in this world. I don't understand your beliefs, your laws." Her eyes felt heavy. She struggled to stay awake.

Koška held her head again. "Open your mouth," she said. "It is time to drink more."

Camryn opened and tasted the combination of acidic and earthy flavors in the lichen water. She swallowed and a calm infused her from her throat to her shoulders and into her heart. Koška lowered her head back to the pillow.

"The void is emptiness," Koška said, her voice sounding as if it were filtered through several padded doors. "When you dream in the Kintala you are entering the void as a projection. But during the test, you will enter the void in reality."

Camryn tried to process what she heard, but it made no sense. "How can it be a dream and reality at the same time?"

"I don't know how to explain it to one who grew up with Agnoses. For the forest people it is accepted that the void exists without meaning."

"Now you are way out in la la land. First you say it is a

dream and then it is real, and now you say it is nothing. Which is it?" Camryn rolled her head from side to side to try to keep awake, but her eyes closed anyway. "Never mind. I'll just keep it as a dream."

"No!" Koška seemed to shout right in her ear and Camryn winced at the noise. "You must understand if you are to live." Camryn struggled to open one eye and saw Koška pacing along the short palette. Then she knelt beside Camryn and shook her shoulders. "Listen. When you are physically in the void you give it meaning. The void takes shape, function, and use based on your feelings, moods, thoughts, and emotions."

"Right, like a dream."

"Lichen mother give me strength," Koška said.

Camryn shot back to a sitting position and screamed as her legs heated like they were burning.

"I'm sorry," Koška said, and the sensation disappeared as quickly as it occurred. "This is how things can feel in the void. Do you see it is not a dream?"

Trying to catch her breath again, Camryn concentrated on not panting. "What the hell did you do to me?"

"I called on fire to do harm. I'm sorry. But if I don't prepare you, you will die."

Camryn felt along her legs. She rolled her pants up to the knee. There was no scaring, nothing to show she had been burned. Yet she would swear she had.

"Okay, okay. I'm awake now. Don't do that again. So, you are saying though it will seem like a dream, it will feel like reality?"

"It will be reality," Koška said. "In the void, you are at the source of creation. You will control fantasy and reality. You will decide what is created, divided, discarded, and recreated."

Camryn's head hurt. She closed her eyes and rubbed her fingers into her forehead. She knew the words Koška was speaking but it was like it was in a language Camryn barely understood. The individual words had meaning but the way they were put together did not.

"Then I'll just decide nothing is real and I'll be okay."

"I wish it were that easy," Koška said. "If I had told you I was going to set your legs on fire but it wouldn't be real, would it have made a difference in the feeling?"

"I don't know. Would it?"

"No. You would still feel like you were on fire. Reality and fantasy are not so easily divided. That is why you must fight."

"But how? I don't understand even half of what you are saying. I have no magical zapper. I've never seen fire or bright blue and green lights come out of my fingers like some wizard. Any chance I get a magic wand or I can learn a spell or something?"

"It doesn't work like that."

Exhausted, Camryn slumped back onto the palette, supporting her head with one hand. "Figures I'd end up in a world that doesn't follow the rules."

"What rules are you talking about?" Koška asked.

"All the movies about magic I've ever watched had spells and castings and wands or staffs or something." Camryn looked Koška in the eyes. "And training. They always had lots of training."

Koška let out a big breath in a loud sigh. "I forget that you are barely sixteen." She pushed back a part of Camryn's hair that shielded half her face.

"Sleep. Go back to sleep. You need your rest."

"No way! Now that I know the next part will be even scarier than my dreams, there is no way I'm sleeping."

"Whether you sleep or not, the tests will come," Koška said. "You are frightened. I understand, but you must sleep. You must regain your strength." She pushed against Camryn's shoulder. "Please lie back and close your eyes. I will do my best to make your dreams happy."

Camryn rolled back to the pallet, but she did not close her eyes. "Has anyone ever died from the Kintala?" she asked. Perhaps death would be welcome. She would be done with all the confusion, done with her search for identity. Finally done —forever.

Koška stroked her arm. "Yes, but I won't let you die."

The soothing voice calmed her.

"It is only those who call death to them who die. They call death because they do not wish to live, because the pain seems unbearable. You must fight, Camryn. You must fight both the darkness and the light. You must fight to live and become your true self."

"Fight the light?" Camryn's eyes fluttered closed and she fought to open them again.

"Yes, while the darkness can bring death, the light brings blindness. You have a choice to balance dark and light. In the past decade, the balance has been skewed. Something has changed in the forest lichen. Something is causing certain factions to become unbalanced. The Abbadon—the evil—is growing."

Camryn struggled to keep her eyes open. "How do you mean? The lichen is evil?"

"No. The lichen is neither good nor evil. It is simply what makes us…different. It enhances our power. But for some of the forest people, their power has gone wild. It's uncontrollable.

"The Ahren are a part of the Mazikeen—a kind of royalty that the ancients called angels. Their children suffered some type of mutation in the past decade. They have been burning bright and dying early. They cannot control the light as they once did. Their illusions can blind. Their illusions can lie. When cast against another, their illusions can be a living death."

Camryn shuddered as she again remembered her dream. "Is Ohar part of the Ahren?"

"Yes." Koška paused for what seemed like a long time. "But I don't think he has the mutation. He is past the age of fifteen where most of the Ahren children die."

Camryn let out a breath she didn't know she was holding. There was another question she wanted to ask about Ohar, but she couldn't remember it now. She was so tired. So very tired.

"And the dark side? Dagger said the Boha'a are the dark side." Camryn's eyes closed and her breathing deepened.

Koška placed a hand lightly on Camryn's head. "The Boha'a lean toward the dark, but not too far. Dagger likes to exaggerate the dark to scare people. The Boha'a are known as the shadow people. But they are not truly evil. Just as the light is not all good, the dark is not all bad. The Boha'a are hedonists, for sure, but not in a way to hurt others." She drew soothing circles on Camryn's forehead.

After a long pause, Koška continued. "Just as with the Mazikeen, there are Boha'a factions who have lost their balance." The Vrag are a subset of the Boha'a who have been lost in the darkness for a decade. They love fear and pain, and their animals have also reflected that same mutation. If you ever run across a Vrag, particularly a Vrag with a black dragon in tow, find protection quickly."

Camryn nodded, unable to fight the slowing of her pulse or the deepening of her breath. She'd never heard of Vrag and the only dragon she'd seen was a white one in her dreams. "Stay," she murmured.

"I will," Koška answered.

I will enter the void with you. Koška spoke in Camryn's mind like she had in the past. *I will try to help you as much as I can.*

"Will you be a cat or a person?" Camryn asked.

I will be an apparition. I will have no power in the void because the test is yours. But I will talk to you.

"How will I find you? How will I find my powers?"

You will find me because you will it. You will find your powers because you will it. Now sleep. Sleep.

Camryn fought the fog in her brain. As she drifted toward the void of identity, she reached for Koška's hand. Instead she found the soft fur of the cat. She sighed and let sleep take her.

WHO ARE YOU?

*The essence of self comes from the source of life. The
more it is sought, the less it is found. Unity is an
acceptance of what one is, not what you wish it to
be. Divide the self and you risk disunity forever.
Use the self to deceive and you risk emptiness.*
--The Fourth Law of the Forest People

amryn floated in space, in a vortex that separated the
sky above and the earth below. All around were

different shades of blue. A shaft of light pierced both above and below. The blue shaft faded to almost white as it reached the sky, and to navy as it reached the earth. She felt no sense of herself. In fact, except for seeing her own legs and arms she would not have thought she was corporal. She listened, but no sound struck her ears.

The absence of sound was definitely weird. Actually, the whole thing was weird. This was completely different than her experience in the dreams. Okay, not so bad. Maybe all she had to do was hang out for a while, keep her mind clear, and it would all be over. Right. If anything Koška said was true, she better enjoy the peace and quiet while she had it.

I'm here.

Camryn felt Koška in her mind. She scanned the area but saw nothing. She saw neither a cat nor a person. She thought of the young girl who had appeared beside her bed.

Good. Very good.

Camryn looked again, and there Koška stood as she'd last seen her but wavy, like a gauze curtain was enveloping her. Camryn could make out the shift dress and bare feet. Her long hair distinguished her delicate features, the color filtered through the filmy covering giving her more of an ethereal look. Like Camryn, she hung in the air, but at a distance.

"Are you real? Or a creation from my thoughts?" Camryn asked.

"Yes!"

Camryn pointed at her. "Not helpful, you know."

Koška giggled. *"Right. I couldn't help myself though."*

"So…now wh—"

Thunder interrupted her. The sky above roiled with lightning. Clouds formed large.

WHO ARE YOU? The question boomed out. Not in a voice like a person, but more like the clouds themselves were addressing her.

"I'm Camryn." She tried to stop her teeth from chattering in fear.

WHO ARE YOU? This time the question was punctuated with lightning.

"I'm Camryn," she shouted. Maybe she had to match the force of the sound.

WHO ARE YOU?

The clouds opened and flying dragons of different colors swopped in from all directions. They headed toward her, talons extended.

Camryn ducked and screamed. The dragons dive bombed her but did not take her. They circled and spiraled. All of them asking the same question, *Who are you? Who are you?*

"What do you want?" Realizing they weren't talking to her, Camryn finally found the confidence to ask. "I'm Camryn. Camryn Painter."

A blood red dragon rose from the earth below. Larger than the others that were circling, the dark talons wrapped around her and it whipped her through the void so fast the chill seared her skin. *Wynbune. Wynbune. Wynbune.* The dragon mocked in her mind. The dragon beat its wings and she felt it rise.

"*Command it!*" Koška yelled from even further away than before.

Then the dragon tipped its head down and dove. Her stomach dropped and her heart seized as she closed her eyes and screamed in terror. Just as she thought they would surely be smashed upon the ground, the dragon pulled up and beat its wings again, pulling her up even higher than before.

"Create your reality!" Koška's command seemed closer this time.

"Reality? This is my freakin' reality."

"Breathe. Camryn. Breathe. The void takes on your emotion. Your fear. Your mood. Create your reality."

Camryn fought against the fear. She sought the redwood forest behind her parents cabin. She thought of blue skies and rays of sunshine filtered through the trees. She hunted for the trillium below them. She breathed deeper and painted the picture in her mind. She pictured herself sitting on an Adirondack chair on the deck, peacefully gazing at the trees, listening for the woodpecker that often woke her early in the morning.

She opened her eyes to the sunshine. It was all exactly how she pictured. She ran her hand along the smooth arm of the chair. Wow. Pretty cool. Now if she could only stay here. She wondered if she could picture her parents and they would appear.

She saw her adopted parents in her mind. She remembered a time when they all shared breakfast on the deck that overlooked the forest. It was her thirteenth birthday. She looked behind her at the sliding door into the cabin, waiting for her mother to appear.

The door opened. "Happy Birthday, sweetheart." Her mother walked toward her with a plate of scrambled eggs and bacon in one hand and orange juice in the other.

"Mom?"

It couldn't be true. She knew her parents were dead. She knew it wasn't real.

She screamed as the dragon dove again.

Once more it pulled out of the dive and headed up. How many more times must she endure this? Obviously the fantasy of her parents wasn't working.

"Command it," Koška said again. *"Create your reality."*

The dragon nosed down and Camryn had had enough.

"Be gone." She shouted at the top of her lungs. "You don't exist. You. Don't. Exist."

The dragon shattered into thousands of pieces and rained red droplets upon the earth below. Camryn hung in the air once more.

She quickly searched for the other dragons. They had all disappeared as well. Interesting. Was that it? Was that the test?

WHO ARE YOU? The clouds boomed thunder again.

Crap! How many times must she endure this question?

"Camryn," she shouted back once more.

WHO ARE YOU?

"Camryn!"

WHO ARE YOU?

"Wynbune!" She finally said, just to shut him up.

She waited, her heart pounding in double time.

Silence.

She let out a breath. Okay. So, maybe they didn't understand her real name.

Ohar appeared before her on a forest path, much like the one on which they'd met after her initial escape. He held out a hand. "Welcome, Wynbune."

Camryn shook her head and backed away. "No way."

"You are Wynbune," he said.

"I am Camryn," she countered.

"And Wynbune," he said.

Neither said anything more, and she was determined not to be the first to speak. Especially since she didn't trust what she saw. Was Ohar really here or not? Did she make him up? If she did, why?

She turned in a circle looking for Koška. Where was that cat when she needed her?

Grr...ow.

Camryn peered between two trees in the direction of the sound. So, she'd changed to cat form and wasn't showing herself to Ohar. Or was Koška a cat now because Camryn thought of her that way? This was so darn confusing.

"You can be both Wynbune and Camryn," Ohar said. "Why must you only be one?"

Camryn turned back. "What are you doing here? Did I call you?"

Ohar canted his head to one side. "I heard your screams. I heard you call out your forest name, Wynbune. It is a beacon to me. I had to come."

"Why?"

"We cannot afford to lose you. You are the hope for our future."

"Who is we?"

"The Mazikeen, of course."

"And what about the rest of the forest people? What about the Boha'a? What about other tribes I don't even know exist?"

"Of course. Of course all of them." He extended his hand to her. "Let me help you, Wynbune. Let me show you the way."

"Um, no. I still have a bad memory of a dream. You called me Lyra, and you…"

Ohar blanched. "I didn't."

"Yes. You did."

"And then what did I do?" he asked.

"I'd really rather not get into that. Let's just say there was a lot of lust going around."

He hung his head. "I'm sorry, Wynbune. I'm truly sorry. I

remember a dream of Lyra. I remember wanting her…in the way you suggest. I do not remember consummating that want. If I did, and it was you, I apologize. This is why I needed to get you to a healer. The Kintala hormones effect us often without us knowing."

He paused and finally looked at her in the eye. "Did I hurt you?"

She shook her head once. "Koška woke me. She stopped the dream before it could go any further."

"Good," he said. "Soon this will be over. Then we can be together in whatever way you desire."

"What if I don't desire to be with you?"

"Please do not tell me you have fallen in love with Dagger. He is a—"

"Stop!" She held her hand to his chest. Whoa! He was real. She suddenly realized he wasn't all shimmery or ghostly like Koška had been before. He was real, like the dragons were real.

"You're real? How can that be?"

She saw his swallow and hesitation.

He dropped his shoulders back and stood tall. "I'm Ahren. We are one with the void. We are often called during the tests."

"To help?" she asked.

He looked away. "No. To judge."

She stepped back again. "I see. And was the whole point of this little charade to get me to admit I was Wynbune?"

"I wasn't called to judge today."

"You just happened to be in the neighborhood, right?"

"I told you, I heard your screams. I had to come."

She wanted to believe him. She had trusted him once. He had seemed kind. But then there was the dream, and the things Dagger said about her birth parents, and…it was all so damn complicated.

"Why didn't Dagger come too?"

Ohar frowned. "You wish for him instead of me?"

"That's not what I said. I'm just asking a question. I'm wondering if he heard the screams too. If he did, why didn't he come too?"

He stared at her for a long time. "He cannot unless you conjure him."

"Conjure? What do you mean? Create?"

"Yes, like you did Koška." He pointed to the trees where the cat still waited.

"So, if I think of him, he will appear?"

"Yes, but…"

"He will be ghostly like Koška," she finished the thought for him.

"Yes."

"But you're not." She paused. "That seems a bit unfair."

He shrugged. "It simply is. The Ahren are one with the void. Other Mazikeen are not…like Koška is not. And there are no Boha'a who can control the void, like the Ahren."

"I see."

"Do you, Wynbune? Do you really see? Do you see how important it is for you to continue? Do you see your destiny? Do you see that you are the chosen? Until you see all of those things, you will be held here."

"How convenient for you." She paced along the path between them. "You just have it all figured out. Who I am. What I'm supposed to do. Down to the last detail, including our marriage even though you will never love me and I will never love you."

"The marriage is not a requirement," he said, his voice almost a whisper. "It is a choice."

"Good to know." She couldn't help but be a bit sarcastic. She was sick and tired of everyone knowing her business, but no one really helping her to figure things out. Well, except for Koška. At least she'd been helpful.

"But I would be honored to be your husband," he continued. "My mother, the queen, has decreed our marriage. But even she cannot force this upon you. It is true I cannot love you like I do Lyra. But I can love you as a man should. I can be a good husband if you allow me."

"How do you know that? How old are you? Seventeen? Eighteen?"

"Eighteen. It is enough to know my duty. It is enough to be your husband and to bring you children."

"Well, I'm only sixteen. And I can't imagine that even at eighteen it will be enough to get married. And let's not even get into the whole children thing. It's not going to happen, okay? Let's get that straight right now. There is no way I'm going to be with someone who is in love with someone else—even if she is dead."

Ohar flinched.

"I'm sorry," she said. "I shouldn't have been so blunt about Lyra. Maybe she's not dead. Maybe she's …oh I don't know…in here somewhere." She gestured around her. Even though it looked like the forest where they met, she knew she was still in the void. She'd learned something.

The forest disappeared and sure enough, she was back hanging between the sky and earth and the shaft of light.

"Geez, these quick shifts can really disorient you," she said. "How do you get used to it?"

"I mostly come here with Woytan. It's different with him."

"He's another Ahren?" she asked.

Ohar smiled and shook his head. "No. He's my bonded thunder dragon."

Camryn immediately scanned the sky, expecting thunder and lightning and the dragons to appear again from the clouds.

"He's not here," Ohar said, his voice low and concerned. "I did not have time to call him when I heard your screams."

Camryn continued to scan, not quite trusting him. "He wouldn't happen to be white would he?"

"Yes…why do you ask?"

Camryn shook her head, as if it would banish the dreams. "The white dragon showed up before you did with your lilacs, and stick, and calling me Lyra."

Ohar groaned. "Lilacs?"

"Um, yeah… Koška told me it wasn't allowed, but it seems that you ignored that little rule too."

"That wasn't me," Ohar said.

"It sure looked like you."

"Yes, I'm sure it did, but I swear I would not have used the lilac stick on you. I would never do that on anyone, especially because of Lyra. I would never…"

He clamped his teeth together and Camryn could hear the angry breaths coming from him. She believed him. She wasn't sure how it was connected to Lyra, but she believed him.

"I will find out who did this. It is someone who entered my dreams and used it against you. That means it was used against me as well."

"Koška suggested it could be…your mother." Camryn turned partially away from him, not sure of his reaction.

"Yes."

It was one word. But a word said with such distaste that Camryn almost felt the burn of his anger. She must be one messed up woman to have her own son not trust her.

"Okay, then," Camryn said. "No need to go there. I'll let you work that out on your own. So, are we done here?"

"Who are you?" Ohar asked, his voice soft, not challenging.

"I am Camryn," she said.

He raised an eyebrow.

"And…I am Wynbune." She struggled with the next part she knew he wanted to hear. "I am the Chameleon."

"Good," he said.

"I don't know what all that means," she continued. "I don't know that I can save your people or any of the people. But I'm willing to try. Is that enough? Because it's all I've got."

Ohar smiled. "You have learned the first lesson of duty to Self. In order to establish autonomy and to find balance, you must understand your inner nature. You must always be in service of the true will."

"True will? Well mine doesn't know what is going on. It's darn confused."

"No, Wynbune. You know it." He fisted his hand over his heart and pounded twice. "In here. You know who you are."

Camryn closed her eyes and tried to just be. She tried to truly accept that nothing was as she imagined just a year ago. She took in a deep breath and let it out. She let her mind range where it would and asked a question to the universe. *Is this the true will?* She wasn't sure if it was a prayer she extended or if she even expected a response. But after only a small amount of time, she felt a lightness of her being, a comforting warmth pass over and through her. She smiled. Yes, she did know the truth of herself.

She opened her eyes. "I *am* the Chameleon." She said it with a sense of wonder, with a sense of rightness this time.

"Welcome, Wynbune/Camryn. Welcome to the forest."

Camryn reached out to take his offered hand and felt fur.

Grr-ow.

She was back in the Alder. Back on her sleeping palette. Sighing she closed her eyes once more.

Sleep. You must sleep before the next test.

A hand stroked her brow. It wasn't Koška this time, but she was too tired to look and see who it might be. She hoped the next test would wait a while.

UNBALANCED

Light and Dark are bonded for eternity. *Desire, envy, and aggression fuel the dark. They dwell in the future. Honesty, benevolence, and kindness fuel the light. They accept the present. The past provides lessons from both. The path of The People is the middle way.*
--The Fifth Law of the Forest People

A column of black smoke roiled in the sky above Camryn. The rocky ground felt solid beneath her feet. The column of smoke churned like a tornado but it wasn't moving forward or backward.

She scanned her environment. Where was she? It wasn't the void—at least not the void as she had experienced it before. It looked like she stood on a plateau in Arizona or New Mexico, or was it Eastern Oregon? Stars twinkled above her and the full moon highlighted a landscape of grey-brown sagebrush, deep purple-topped heather, and grey-green grasses that stretched as far as the eye could see. Only the occasional shadowed juniper tree broke up the rolling landscape. In the distance, an orange glow at the horizon may have been the lights of a small town—but nothing in the landscape or the sky was so descriptive as to give her bearings.

Camryn looked toward the smoky column and blinked. The column now served as a focal point around which it appeared stars were moving in a circle—like you might see in a long camera exposure at night. Definitely not reality, she decided. Not the void, but not earth. She took a deep breath and prepared for whatever would be the next test in the Kintala.

Dagger's face appeared in the column, larger than life—like the giant face in the Wizard of Oz. Then he walked out of it, his normal size but with each step smoke trails curled off him forming a vaporous aura in his wake. His smoky hand stretched toward her as if offering to take hers.

Camryn took a step back. This couldn't be the real Dagger. Ohar told her he couldn't enter the void without her asking. She didn't remember asking.

Dimples showed in his gauzy face. He opened his mouth to laugh and puffs of black smoke spewed with each guffaw.

"Are you real or did I accidentally call you?" She asked.

The smoky Dagger laughed even more. "You want me, Camryn." It was a pronouncement, not a question.

"No. I do not." She crossed her arms as if they could offer protection against him.

Dagger took three quick bounds toward her, a murky mist trailing behind. He wrapped her in smoke-filled arms that felt solid and smothering. "Yes, you do. You must learn to use and enjoy the powers of darkness. The first is desire."

His mouth sought hers and she pushed against him, but what was solid before suddenly became fluid and her hands went through the smokiness of his torso. Yet his lips felt solid as he kissed her.

"No! I. Do. Not." She fisted her hands and brought her arms and crossed them hard across her face, cutting his head from his torso. The orange glow from the horizon formed a protective aura around her. Dagger reformed again and laughed, but he was now unable to penetrate her shield.

"Good show of aggression." He clapped his hands slowly and thunder boomed with each clap. "Do you know what you did?"

"I stopped you," she said, lifting her chin, proud of herself. "And I suspect I can do worse."

"Much worse," he said. "And you must learn to harness those dark powers and use them for survival."

"I won't hurt anyone."

"We will see." Dagger lifted his arms and called to the moon. The language he used was unfamiliar to Camryn, yet she understood what he was doing.

Large rocks hurtled toward her out of the swirling stars behind him, growing larger by the second. Intuitively, she changed her stance with one foot slightly behind the other for balance and she raised her right arm and cocked it at a right angle in front of her face for protection. She fisted her left hand and swung it forward, opening her hand with the palm facing the coming onslaught. "No!" she shouted. A shaft of blue and white light met the boulders exploding them into thousands of smaller pieces that rained in the distance.

Camryn shook from the effort. She'd never done anything like that before. "How did I—"

Before she could finish her question, what appeared to be a giant fireball hurtled from the center of the circle. "Douse!" she shouted twirling as fast as she could in a circle. Large waves rose around her and covered the fireball. She hunched close to the ground as the waves drenched both her and Dagger.

The wind picked up and swirled around them. Camryn's teeth chattered as her wet clothes absorbed the cold, harsh wind. She could see Dagger was now clothed in furs, oblivious to the cold. The clouds opened above her and large snowflakes fell and swirled in the wind until she could no longer see Dagger or the landscape. She could only see white and her entire body shook in the cold.

Unable to talk or move, Camryn knew there was nothing she could do. She had no training in how to get out of this. She could barely believe she'd taken care of the boulders and the fireball. The Kintala had finally bested her. She closed her eyes and wished that if she had to die, she could at least be warm. *Heat. Heat. Heat.* The unconscious chant became the focus of everything.

The earth beneath her shook and she fell to the ground. Small holes opened up around her, bubbling with hot lava. Just great. Now I've created a volcano and I'll burn to a crisp before I die. She tried to think of something else to stop this latest test, but her mind could no longer form thoughts.

"Anger!" Dagger shouted from a distance. "Use your anger. Get mad at the universe. Throw your anger at it."

Camryn had no anger. She couldn't even manage fear. She closed her eyes. She was so tired. Tired of the tests. Tired of the expectations. Maybe if she could rest for just a while, she could get up the energy to be angry. She fingered the dreamcatcher that still hung about her neck and thought of her mother, then slipped into oblivion.

When she woke again, Dagger was sitting beside her. He looked like his normal self—at least as normal as Dagger could look. He brushed a hand across her forehead, moving her hair out of eyes.

"I know what you want more than anything else," Dagger said.

Camryn sat up and noticed they were beneath a lichen-covered tree, much like the tree where he had kidnapped her from Ohar. How long ago was that? She couldn't remember. Was it days? Weeks? How long had she been in the Kintala?

She shook her head. "I don't even know what I want more than anything else except for whatever this lesson is to be over."

Dagger slowly gestured as if drawing a large rectangle in front of him. A silvery sheen, like a mirror with no edges appeared. Dagger stood and pulled her up to stand beside him. His hand was solid in hers. He reeled her into his rock-hard chest.

She caught her breath. "Your...but you can't be...you—"

"I'm here just like Ohar was here before." He continued to hold her tight against him.

"But he said—" She pushed on his chest and he let go, but stayed near.

"He says a lot of things that are not true. The Boha'a long ago learned how to penetrate the void. We couldn't leave that power only to the Ahren who were making changes in the other dimensions that effect us all."

Camryn rubbed her temples. She was getting really tired of this feud between Boha'a and Mazikeen. She didn't understand where it came from or why everyone just couldn't get along.

Dagger took her hand again, this time with a soft touch. "Let me show you what you want more than anything."

"It's *not* you. So don't even try anything."

He laughed. "So confident, are you? Not to worry. This time it's not all about my desires. It's about yours."

He pulled her through the mirrored surface. It wavered for a moment like a watery dimple when she dived into a pool. They exited near the cabin where she'd lived with her adopted parents.

Dagger moved his hand, palm up, across the landscape before them. "This is what you want."

Her mother and father came out of the cabin to a grill on the patio. They were laughing, enjoying preparing dinner together. They looked real. There was no fuzziness in the picture, no two-dimensionality. She rubbed her eyes and stared. What was the trick? There had to be a trick.

Her father lit the grill and then her mother uncovered the red, foil-covered plate she held. Camryn heard the foil crinkling, as her mother worked it into a small ball.

"Best kabobs ever, Bliant." Her father kissed her mother's cheek and took the plate, expertly placing each stick on the grill. There were six total.

"Where's Camryn?" He asked.

Her mother looked toward the forest where she stood with Dagger.

She pointed directly to them. "Camryn, who is that with you?"

Camryn held her breath. How could it be? They saw her *and* Dagger? This wasn't real. It couldn't be real. They couldn't see her. In fact, they weren't alive. They had died in an accident. She knew that was real. She'd had a year in Starlight Center to prove it.

"Go on," Dagger said, taking her hand and stepping forward. "Introduce me. This is what you want, isn't it?"

Camryn shook her head. "No. Take me back. It's a trick. I know it's a trick."

"No trick," he said, and pulled her forward again.

Her mother approached them and gave her a hug. "Where have you been? It's been a long time."

Camryn let tears escape her lashes as she held on tight. She couldn't speak. She'd never believed in a million years that she would see her parents again. Her mother's touch felt so good. It felt real. It felt right.

Her mother gently extricated herself form Camryn's hold. "Are you okay, sweetheart? Is something wrong?" Her finger wiped away a tear that lingered on Camryn's cheek. "I know it's been awhile since you went away, but your back now." She hugged her again and quickly released her. "Okay?"

Camryn nodded, but she wasn't sure at all that anything was okay or ever would be again.

Dagger reached out his hand and offered it to her mother. "I'm Dagger. Glad to meet you. Camryn has told me so much about you."

"I can see that you are Boha'a. How is Abrani Daj? Is she still well?"

Dagger smiled broadly. "Yes, and if she'd known we were coming I'm sure she would have sent her greetings."

"Just a minute." Her mother turned away. "Let me get my

husband. He'll want to meet you too." She walked back toward the grill.

"NO!. No. No. No." Camryn said. "It's not real. It's not real." She closed her eyes and searched for the true will. She had found it with Ohar when she accepted her true self. She could find it again. She would learn the truth.

"Camryn, don't do this." Dagger's voice was fading as she turned into herself and put the question to the universe. "You can have this and Ohar and me and anything else you desire. You can have it all. Just open yourself to it and I will teach you."

"No," she whispered. "No. It's not natural. It's not right."

When she opened her eyes again, she was back in the void and the black tornado of smoke roiled again before her. Dagger's face appeared and disappeared again and again. "It's yours for the taking. To survive, you must learn to take what you need as much as you give. That is the balance of dark and light."

"No," she said again. "It's not balance for me." She wrapped her arms around herself and pulled in, bending slightly as if she had to hold onto herself to keep reality in focus. "I loved my parents. I know the difference between reality and fantasy. That wasn't real because I wasn't real. In my life with my parents I had never been able to control my changes. Yet, when my mother greeted me I did not change into her."

"Because you have grown. Because you have learned control," the dark mass boomed.

"No, because it was a partial memory. I don't know how you extracted it or why, but it wasn't real and I don't want it. It is nothing like the real thing."

The lightning worked between the sky and the ground in the void and Dagger again materialized out of the smoke. Then the scene changed to one just outside a large tent on the edge of the forest.

Her feet felt solid ground again as she faced him. "Where am I now?"

"You are at the edges of the Boha'a camp." He pointed toward the tent. "This is my home. Come." He gestured for her to enter the tent.

She shook her head no. There was no way she was going inside anywhere with him. She didn't trust him one bit. She knew there was some type of attraction to him that she didn't understand. But she knew it wasn't real. In fact, she wasn't sure whatever she was experiencing right now was real either.

His hand extended to her. "I was wrong," he said. "You are more pure than I imagined. You are as pure as the Ahren of old."

Camryn ignored his offered hand and didn't budge. She wasn't sure what he wanted now, but she suspected it was another trick.

He smiled. The dimples in his cheek deepened. "You don't trust me."

"Ya think?"

He laughed. "I'm sure I deserved that."

She looked again at the tent and then back at the forest. She backed up a couple of steps and angled her body slightly so that she could run if needed.

"There is no need to be afraid of me," Dagger said. "I won't harm you. I won't make you do anything you don't want to do."

"And I should believe that, why?"

Dagger's lips quirked up in a smirk. "You've proven your strength," he said. "I don't want to deal with you throwing spears of light or fire at me if you get angry."

"Yeah, right. Like you couldn't stop me."

His mouth no longer smiled. He looked her straight in the eye. "I'm not sure I could," he said. "Your powers are way beyond mine. The only thing I have that you don't is control and practice. If you decided to really unleash your power to harm me, there would be no way for me to stop you." He paused and then opened his mouth, but said nothing. He closed it again and looked away.

Camryn looked down at her hands. How did she do that? Was it real? Now that she was in somewhat normal surroundings, it all felt like a dream—kind of surreal. Except for her parents. They had felt very real. Too real. She choked back the pain of seeing them and knowing they were dead.

"Where was I?" She asked, her voice low. "How did you make that happen?"

"I can ride eight of the ten dimensions of the forest network," he said, as if it were as easy as driving a car.

"Whoa." She held up a hand to stop him. "No need to make up stories. I'm full up to here." She waved a palm above her head. "I can't take anymore fantasy versus reality stuff right now. Besides I'm not stupid. There are only four dimensions. I learned that in my studies. Yes, that whole space-time thing is kind of wonky, but even Einstein said no time travel to the past was possible."

"This isn't time travel," he said. "This is understanding that the universe isn't linear." He took a stick and drew a piece of bread in the dirt and then divided it into many very small slices. "Space-time is not linear. It is warped and folds back on itself. This creates an infinite number of historical possibilities. You can, in effect return to a past that is close to your experience but different enough to be what you want."

She shook her head, as if it would help the fuzziness to

congeal. "That doesn't make sense. Dead is dead and no one can undo that in any time…I mean space or time."

"Yes, in your experience your parents died. I'm sorry that is truth for you. But that is not true throughout space and time. The other six dimensions are curled up into a space so small that the Agnoses don't notice them. But the Forest People, through their experience with the lichen and their evolution can manipulate those dimensions to some extent—ride them if you will. When these dimensions curl and warp, we encounter every single possible history, each with its own probability. In the one where I took you, your parents didn't die, and the Agnoses and Forest People interact more easily as one society."

Camryn blew out a big breath. He was just trying to confuse her. In fact, she wasn't even sure if she was talking to the real Dagger now. For all she knew she was dreaming, or still in the void, or …well, she didn't know all the other possibilities. It was giving her one big headache.

"It just doesn't make sense," she argued. "You can't physically change so much, you can't manipulate it. You can't travel it. Even if you could. DNA doesn't change so quickly."

"But it does," Dagger countered. "How do you think the lichen covers you and transports you? How do you think you can travel within the tree network even up to a platform without significantly changing?"

"Okay, okay." She rubbed at her eyes, hoping maybe at some point she'd open them and just be back on the platform in the alder. Nope. No such luck. "Okay," she said again, accepting she was still stuck here talking to Dagger—whether he was real or not. "I know something happens, and I don't understand it. But it doesn't mean I'm traveling in other dimensions or anything."

She rolled her shoulders backward a couple of times to shrug off that first memory of the lichen covering her. That whole lichen thing was not fun. But she had to admit it was weird how it took her places. It felt like she imagined the Star Trek transporter must feel. It was like everything fragmented into thousands of parts and then somehow united again in just the right way to make her whole somewhere else. She didn't exactly feel it happen, but she was aware of it happening. If that made sense.

" DNA is only one dimension that defines who we are, or defines what powers we inherit," Dagger continued. "The Forest People have learned that more important is non-DNA cellular transmission of traits—behavioral traits and symbolic communication is also inherited. How do you think you knew, what to do with the hurtling boulders? How did you know what to do with the fireball? How did you know to use your mind to communicate and control your power, when you couldn't speak?"

"I don't know. I didn't think, I just reacted." She said.

"Exactly," Dagger agreed. "You were never taught those skills, but they are a part of you passed down from your Mazikeen mother and your Quatcho father. You've never been taught how to use it. It's instinctive. For the Forest People, that instinctual knowing and acting is key to our survival."

"Okay, so maybe I can open my mind to other dimensions and a different way of inheriting genes and traits and all that stuff, but it still doesn't explain everything. There has to be similarities too. There has to be a string I could follow, if I knew how, that makes the change slight from one dimension to another. It can't just be completely different. Right?" She pounded her fist against her thigh. "Something has to be real, otherwise I'm going to go crazy."

"There are similarities that can be traced," he agreed.

"But, my parents didn't know about the Forest People. They

didn't know I was a Chameleon. They didn't know I had powers beyond the changes. They didn't know how to help me."

"Are you sure?"

"Yes….I…" Camryn paused. No. She wasn't so sure now. Her mother did mention that on her sixteenth birthday she would take her to someone to help her. Who could that have been? Her mother always told her that she had a gift and would learn to use it at the right time. "Oh no." She suddenly felt cold, as disbelief worked its ghostly fingers down her back.

Dagger leaned forward and hugged her tight.

She leaned her forehead against his chest. "My mother did know. She knew something. She kept promising it would make sense, but then…everything happened…and…" Her eyes misted as she realized her mother simply ran out of time. She had no way to know she would die before she could help Camryn. "Why didn't she tell me. Why…" She buried her head in his chest, hoping to staunch the tears before they fell.

He stroked her back and kept saying, "Just let it go, Camryn. You have proven yourself more than any other in the Kintala. You have proven you are the chosen."

She refused to give in to her grief once again. She didn't understand much about this world, but she did want to learn more. More than that she wanted to help.

Camryn raised her face to look up at Dagger. She caught her breath as his eyes softened. He placed his index finger at the edge of her lash and drew a tear onto it.

"The tears of an Ahren are always tears of love," he said, his voice soft and inviting. "The tears of the Chameleon are also strong and purifying. Never fear crying, Camryn. It is a sign of strength to feel, to care so deeply."

His finger moved beneath her chin and tilted it slightly. Her breath quickened and her mouth opened. All she could think about was how much he understood her, how much he'd shared with her, how much she wanted him. She raised up on her toes and gently placed her hand on his neck, pulling his lips toward hers.

She wanted this. More than any other time, she knew now she wanted him.

SURVIVAL

"The Kintala has ended." Koška wiped the tears from Camryn's eyes as she came awake. "Are you okay?"

Camryn could only nod. She had no words to express her feelings. All that happened. All that she had learned. It was overwhelming.

Koška shifted and sniffed the air. "My step-brother comes. I must leave."

Camryn grabbed Koška wrist. "Thank you," she whispered. "Thank you for staying with me."

Koška nodded then quickly shifted to her cat self and jumped the branches down the tree, moving into the shadowed woods.

"Camryn?" Camryn covered her ears at Dagger's resounding voice. She shushed loudly with a finger to her lips.

"Sorry." Dagger's voice was several decibels lower. "I forget finishing the Kintala is like recovering from a hangover. May I come up?"

Camryn sighed. She could already hear him climbing. "Does it really matter what I answer?" She whispered.

His head appeared over the edge of her pallet. He grinned. "Nope. Just being polite." He pulled himself over the edge and sat cross-legged in front of her. "Abrani Daj told me your Kintala is done and you survived. I must say I'm happy."

Camryn cocked her head to one side. "Was there any doubt I'd survive?"

Dagger's cheeks dimpled. "I guess not." He winked. "I suppose now that you've passed though the Kintala you aren't so hot for me anymore."

"That's right," she lied. She looked at him sideways. Did he also remember everything that happened in the smoky cyclone? In the void? Her parents? The kiss? No. If he did he would act differently, wouldn't he? She swallowed. Nothing is ever as it seems.

Camryn held her head high and stood. If he brought it up, she'd deal it with it then. Until that happened, she would assume it was a dream, or another dimension. Anyway it wasn't real for this present time.

She had felt the pull to kiss him as he climbed to greet her. It wasn't the roaring insistent passion begging for immediate satiation she'd felt just before the Kintala started. Instead, it was more like a constant thrum just below the surface. She hoped it was something that would dissipate more with each passing day. Dagger was not her type and there was no way she was going to be with him in that way no matter what her body wanted.

"Would you take me somewhere if I asked?"

Dagger swallowed. "You want to go back to Ohar, don't you?"

"No. I want to see my father." She paused and looked him in the eye. "I know you can take me. I want to see him. Now."

Dagger looked away and expelled a big breath. "Before you can do that you need to learn how to wield your magic."

"Learn? As in study? I thought we each had magic within us. It is defined. It just is."

Dagger snorted. "Sure it is, but if you have no control you can hurt people. You can hurt yourself."

"So is this about spells, and calling the four elements and making circles on the ground?" Camryn remembered reading about such things, but nothing in this world indicated anyone used that stuff. It was more fairy tale than the forest people. Oops. The forest people turned out to be true. She swallowed and cast her eyes down. How much more was there to learn to understand?

Dagger's hand lightly touched her shoulder and she looked up into his eyes.

"All that stuff you mentioned. That's ceremonial stuff. It isn't really needed. It just provides focus. We use some of that to teach the children because their minds are always wandering. And lately…since the mutations started…when a mind wanders a tree can burn, or a house can blow up, or a boiling geyser can suddenly appear."

"Not good," Camryn said. She definitely didn't want to cause any of those things. All she wanted to do was find her father and get him out of whatever prison the Mazikeen had fashioned for him.

"Right," Daggered said. "And your powers are even more than a child's. So, I can teach you some focus tools."

Camryn wasn't sure she wanted Dagger to teach her anything. Her last memory of him, during the Kintala, was not of someone in control and not of the kind of magic she wanted to learn.

She stepped away from him. He raised a brow in question.

"I'm not exactly comfortable with you," she said.

He stepped forward. "I won't hurt you."

She stepped back another pace. "Don't crowd me. Get out of my personal space."

He stayed in place. "What happened? Something I did during the Kintala?"

"I'd rather not talk about it."

"It may help if you do. I may be able to help you interpret it."

"No." She was not backing down on this. There was absolutely no way she would put into words what happened or how she felt. If he didn't already know, there was definitely no way she was going to put any ideas into his head.

"Is there someone else who can teach me? Someone who is not a guy?" She worried her bottom lip. "I just think I'll feel better with a girl right now."

"Like Koška?"

She sucked in a breath. "You knew she was with me in the Kintala?"

"I know a lot about my sister." His jaw tightened and his eyes narrowed. "I know a lot of things about many of the forest people."

Camryn took a step back. "How?"

He laughed. His seriousness turning to that devil-may-care attitude she thought he sported as a mask. "I am a Boha'a thief, remember? Thieves have all kinds of knowledge."

She pushed at his shoulder, playfully. He grabbed her wrist and held it tight. "And I know about you, Camryn. I know more about you than you do about yourself."

She refused to back away or to show any sign of fear. "Then

you know the most important thing I can do is to find my father and free him. He is the only one who can tell me the truth about my past. He *may* be the only one who can tell me the truth about my future."

He released his hold on her wrist and stepped away, shaking his head. "It's too dangerous. The place they are keeping your father is not safe. It's not like here. It's not part of the Redwoods. It's cold. High on a mountain. You could easily freeze to death if you don't accidentally slip and fall."

"I don't care. I have to go," Camryn said. "I need to see him. I don't know what I'm supposed to do as the Chameleon, but I know that it begins with freeing my father and learning more about my parents and their people."

Dagger looked to the east and shook his head.

"If you won't help me, I'll find someone who will. "

"Who? Ohar?" Dagger spit on the ground in disgust. "You expect him to tell you where the Mazikeen have imprisoned your father?"

Camryn rolled her eyes. "I'm not an idiot. Of course I'm not going to ask him. But I will find someone who knows. Maybe Abrani Daj." She moved to seek the old woman.

Dagger moved in front of her. "No. Don't go to Abrani."

"Why not?"

His face colored and he looked away. "Just. Don't."

Camryn paused. For the first time since she'd met Dagger, it seemed he was actually embarrassed. Something wasn't right here. She stared.

"She's…She'll want you to…Look, just trust me. She is *not* the one who can help you in this. There are rules. Rules you don't understand about what happens after the Kintala. Who you will be with next. Who you will…"

"What? What rules? Who I will be with? You mean I can't be with Abrani Daj? Why not?"

"Ah, crzzl." Dagger's breath escaped with the swear word. "Look. Because you completed the Kintala here, it's kind of like you're now a part of the Boha'a tribe. That means Boha'a customs. Boha'a rules."

Camryn squinted her eyes and looked to the side at him. "And that's bad because?"

"Because the first man you see will be the one you engage with the balvan ceremony." The words came out in a rush. "Not that I believe all that crzzl, but Abrani Daj does and if you go looking for her before you know it, we will be stuck in a tent with a guard until the deed is done."

"Balvan?"

"Yeah. Until I've…you're…well…until we have sex."

Camryn yanked her arm away from his grasp. "What the hell? That's barbaric. No one in the 21st century does that. I can't believe it." She paced as if walking it out would make it a lie. "Don't even think it. There is absolutely no way in hell you and I are ever going to… " she sputtered. "I don't even want to kiss you. I don't even want to be with you as a friend. I don't even…."

Dagger guffawed, then he laughed so hard he held his stomach.

Camryn stomped her foot. "It's not funny."

"Um, yeah it is." His cheeks dimpled as he barely held back another chuckle.

He took a step toward her. "I wouldn't mind … being with you, you know in that way."

She refused to back up. He was just trying to unbalance her, confuse her. She raised her chin. "It's never going to happen."

He stepped closer again. "I wouldn't mind kissing you either."

She held her ground. "That's not going to happen either."

He stepped so close their lips were within inches of each other. "Don't even think it," she said between locked teeth.

Dagger slowly drew two fingers down from her temple and across her cheek.

She took in an involuntary breath.

His index finger sketched her closed lips. Not once, but twice. "I'm thinking it," he whispered. "I'm definitely thinking it."

Camryn swallowed. She was unable to move and unable to take her eyes from his.

After what seemed like several minutes, but was probably only seconds, she gathered her strength and said. "My father. Are you going to help me or not?"

Dagger sighed and stepped back. He took her hand. "Come on. I'll help. I can't go with you because I'd endanger you if the Mazikeen learned I was there. I should be shot for putting you in danger like this, but I can see that whether I tell you how to find him or not you'll find a way to at least search for him."

"Thanks." Camryn kissed his cheek.

He pulled her hand and headed toward his tent. "Don't thank me. By the time you get there you'll probably hate me. Now listen carefully. I'm only going to tell you this once and you have to believe everything I say. It could mean the difference between life and death."

Camryn stumbled after him, trying to keep up. "Slow down or I'll trip," she yelled.

He stopped abruptly. "Sorry. I just don't want to do this."

"I know." Camryn started forward in the direction he had been taking her, setting a more normal pace. "Go ahead."

"First. You have to remember you are now one with the forest," Dagger said. "You will be traveling the interdimensional circuits of the gateway trees. These circuits can move you to any forest, any mountaintop or meadow, anywhere in the world there is a tree. The ancient ones call these trods, but it's nothing like a trail or a path as you know it. In fact, it feels more like your entire body is being taken apart and reassembled. You can move through time and space. Right now you will only move through space."

Camryn shivered with the memory of the lichen covering her, suffocating her.

"The lichen provides you breath," he continued as if reading her fears. "Don't fight it and it will protect you."

"That's easier said than done," she replied.

He stopped and faced her. "You have to welcome it, breathe it in." He closed his eyes and inhaled deeply. A green cast covered his face, then mottled quickly along his arms and torso.

"No!" Camryn stepped back, letting go of his hand for fear it would take her too.

Dagger expelled his breath and the lichen retreated even quicker than it had come upon him. "You can control it. It can keep you warm in the coldest climate if you know how to welcome it." He grabbed her shoulders and squeezed. "It's important you understand this, Camryn. You will need it where you are going."

She nodded, but still unsure she could ever welcome that into her body again.

"You will be traveling the circuit in the eighth dimension."

"Not the dimension stuff again," she mumbled. "It was way too complicated the first time."

"You seemed to accept it during the Kintala," he said.

She stopped her forward motion and yanked on his arm.

"You knew! Damn you, Dagger. You *were* there in the void. You know exactly what happened between us. My powers, my concerns." She lowered her head. "My parents." Her breath came in short spurts as the anger built on his betrayal. He even knew about…her cheeks warmed as she remembered that kiss. How dare he play with her! How dare he pretend her experience was outside his knowledge. "You played me," she said, her teeth locked together lest she spit at him. "How can I trust you? How can I trust anything or anyone? First Ohar. Now You. Is there anyone in this forest who doesn't know every move I make? Is there anyone who can be truthful? Is there anyone who really gives a damn about reality."

Dagger stood, unmoving. She could see his body was tense —but not in the spring-at-prey sort of way. It was more like he was holding back.

"I give a damn," he said. "This isn't all about you, Camryn. It's about our entire world. It's about the forest network and the people and the destruction of everything we know. That's what's before you. And if it takes me entering the void or interrupting your Kintala, I'll do it. I'll do it because I'm going to make damn sure you don't kill yourself by accident. And if that takes betrayal, not being completely truthful, or meeting whatever ethical standard you seem to have about life. That's tough. I'm a thief. Remember? I take what I need. Period."

Camryn stared at him. She had no words to rebut. She wasn't sure whether to admire him or hate him.

Dagger's shoulders dropped and he sighed. "Do you want help with your finding your father or not?"

She nodded. Unwilling to form words or ask questions where she couldn't trust the veracity of the answers anymore.

"My purpose is to keep you safe. The last thing I want is for you to be forever lost in some alternate history line." Then he stepped inside the tent without turning to see if she followed.

She grabbed the flap and stepped in after him. The last thing *she* wanted was to be forever swallowed in green lichen. Camryn scanned the interior. She was taken by the neatness and homey feel of the temporary structure. It was unlike the pup tents she had ever experienced while camping with her parents in national parks around the United States. Set on a raised wooden deck, the tent was furnished with a comfortable-looking double bed at the back of the tent with lighted lanterns on either side. Colorful rugs were placed at the foot of the bed and near two camp chairs in the middle of the room, with canvas footstools in front of them. Each chair also had a quilted throw draped across it. Separating the chairs was a small oval table. Toward the front of the large tent space was a basin placed on a wooden table with a lantern hung beside it.

"Wow. I didn't know tent living could be so nice."

Dagger rooted through a pile of ragged pieces of leather and fur. "It is home and it can be disassembled in about an hour and moved if needed. We move frequently, as we are travelers and somewhat outcast from the People. We have no permanent home in the forest."

Camryn joined him near the basket. "How long have you been here?"

"Eighteen months this time. This is the longest I've been in one place in my memory." Dagger pulled out a mahogany-brown furred tunic streaked with black and gold and held it up for inspection. "This was my sister's," he said, throwing it in her direction. "You'll need some things to keep you warm." A piece of leather followed to tie the tunic around her waist. He delved again into the pile and then threw a pair of goggles out and a furred hat that would fit close to her head.

Dagger looked back at her, his eyes moving from her face to her feet. "You'll need something to keep your legs and feet warm." He moved to another part of the tent, closer to the bed, and rummaged through some type of chest until he flung more leather and fur bands toward the pile he was making near her.

Camryn picked them up. "I'm to be a female Robin Hood then?" she asked.

Dagger tilted his head and furrowed his brow. "A what?"

"Never mind. It's an Agnoses thing from television," she said.

"Put on the tunic and tie the leather thong around your middle," he instructed. "I'll help with the leggings and coverings for your shoes."

He kneeled in front of her and wrapped the fur strips around her legs then tied them with more leather strips. "Tell me if these are too tight. I don't want to cut off any circulation."

Her skin sizzled at his touch. She could barely speak. "It's… fine," she finally eeked out and stepped away. "Tell me more about the dimensions."

Dagger stepped around her and moved toward the door. "Have a seat." He pointed toward the camp chairs. "Tea? You might as well have something warm because you'll find this hard to take in."

Camryn laughed. "Right. Like everything else has been easy so far. Lichen taking me over, traveling through a tree, experiencing the Kintala, finding light can come out of my fingers and I can call up waves of water without even knowing what I'm doing. Yeah, everything's just peachy."

He touched her shoulder. "I'm sorry it's all happening so fast, Camryn. I'm sure it's scary."

She looked at him, once more unable to answer. Why was he

suddenly being so nice. So understanding. This did not help her keep her distance.

He cleared his throat. "Back in a minute. I have to go to the cooking tent for hot water." Then he left her alone.

Camryn pinched herself. Yep. Still seemed to be real. Even though the Kintala was over, she couldn't help but wonder if this was one of the most realistic dreams she'd ever had, or some new drug Dr. Frenelli had given her. Although it all felt very real, it was unbelievable. She rubbed her forehead. Was it possible for your brain to take in too much? And if your brain gives up, are you left forever in some fantasy world?

Soon Dagger returned. Steam rose from a small ceramic teapot that seemed out of place in his tent. The orange and yellow roses around the bottom matched the roses on the two teacups he also carried on the tray.

"Pretty fancy having tea served in a tent," Camryn said. "Even if it is a fancy tent by camping standards."

Dagger poured the hot liquid into a cup and handed it to her. "The Boha'a are civilized, in spite of what the Mazikeen might have told you."

"The only Mazikeen I've met is Ohar," she said. She closed her eyes and let the spicy aroma of the tea soothe her before taking a sip. "Mmmmm." She opened her eyes.

"Feeling better?" He asked.

She set her teacup down. "A little. But I'm anxious to understand all this dimension stuff. I mean, I did take some physics but that was more math based, not really practical. Not that anything in your world is practical."

He chuckled. "I feel the same way about the Agnoses world." He stood and walked toward the same chest where he'd taken out the rags and clothes before. "I may have something that can help. It's from our ancient text. It's something we learn as a children in a kind of rhyme to get the dimensions in our head."

She heard rustling. Then he placed seven pieces of parchment in front of her. "There is one for each dimension beginning with the fourth."

She read them in silence.

FOURTHS ARE ONE DIRECTION
Walk the forest path from the past to the future.
Begin as a babe and end as a teacher.
In only one direction may your travels take.
To step backward is a deathly mistake.

FIFTHS FOR INDIVIDUAL DECISION
Fourths have parallels at each junction
Decisions are made in order to function
If you pass the place, no fifths are made
If you take the branch prepare to be paid.

SIXTHS NETWORK THE TREES
Fourths and fifths require a path
But sixths allow different math
Every branch is an alternate parallel
Trust the trees for trods will serve you well.

Camryn rubbed fingers at her temples. "I think this is beyond what my brain can take in. Can I get a copy of the tree mapping?" Camryn asked.

"Well no. There isn't really a physical map, but the lichen working in your body talks to the trees and the gateway trees are nodes of a network that knows the map."

"So the sixth dimension allows me to get to places which are not directly connected to my path?"

Dagger finished his tea and stood in front of her. "Yes, you've got it. Only four rhymes to go."

SEVENTHS ARE WHOLE
Get out of the trees and see the whole.
Then it will be clear where you can go.
Stand on the edge and see the plan.
Then you can move from stand to stand.

Camryn could feel her eyes drooping. She closed them for just a minute and tried to concentrate. "So, I'm guessing that if the seventh dimension of the network allows me to see another forest, then it seems we can travel anywhere now. Isn't that enough dimensions?"

"In the seventh, the map is from one forest to another known forest. The eighth dimension allows you to travel to forests that are unknown." He recited the eighth from memory.

EIGHTHS TAKE FAITH
If you are unsure of your route.
All known forest trods will be moot.
Speak the ancient name to the mother tree.
The grace of the lichen will safely guide thee.

"This is how you will travel to Eighre Terrace," he said. "Because you have not been there, you do not have a mental map that tells you how to traverse from one forest to another—how to make the decisions at the junctures. Also, you do not know where along the path the gateway tree for Eighre Terrace lies. So, you must rely on travel in the eighth dimension. You must place your faith in the lichen."

Camryn shivered at the thought of trusting a tree network that was the equivalent of some physics equation she could never master. "That sounds spooky. How come I can't just get a map of all the forests in relation to each other first?"

"In time, anyone who is of the People can absorb that map in their heart and their head will follow. You are of the People, Camryn, but because you haven't lived here it seems foreign to you right now. But once you start traveling, it will become second nature."

Camryn stretched her hands and arms above her to keep sleep from claiming her. "Somehow, I doubt it," she said. "If all I need is to call to the eighth dimension then let's stop there. I'm sure the ninth-dimension is like where God lives, right?"

Dagger chuckled and took her finished teacup to the wash-stand. "No, not God, just very old forest people who have innate trust in the lichen. A ninth-dimensional being becomes one with the gateway tree and can see a map of all the forests and where they are in relation to each other in space and time. Someone who can travel in the ninth-dimension doesn't even have to think of the destination to get there directly. Her heart beats as one with the gateway."

"Wow! Can you do that?" Camryn asked.

Dagger shook his head. "Abrani Daj is the only one I've ever known to do it. And she is over 500 years old. It doesn't come easily."

"Okay." Camryn said the word slowly, drawing it out. "I'm not getting a good feeling about this. It means trusting something I can't see, getting suffocated again by lichen, and maybe getting lost." She swallowed hard. "Lost forever you said. Are you sure there is no other way for me to get to Eighre Terrace?"

Dagger took her hands in his. "You won't be lost as long as you focus on where you want to go. I'll make sure you have it, you just need to keep it in your mind."

"How can I keep something in my mind I don't understand and I've never seen?"

"Faith." Dagger closed is eyes and a glow, an aura of blue and green and orange radiated from him.

Camryn's mouth opened in awe. Was that magic or something else?

After a couple minutes the aura dissipated and Dagger opened his eyes. "Faith is what you have when there is nothing else. If you maintain your faith, you will be protected."

Camryn shook her head. She'd never been a faith-in-what-she-didn't-understand kind of girl. If anything she was sure that God had abandoned her. What kind of God would make someone like her—someone who had no control over who she is or even how she looked?

She stared hard at Dagger. "Are you an angel?"

"Hardly." He laughed so hard she thought he might have a seizure. He took her hands in his. "Listen. I showed you my aura so you would know I am not all evil. I am not all darkness and smoke as you experienced in the Kintala."

She slid her hands away from his. She'd rather not remember him as some kind of smoke monster. She'd almost forgotten that. She'd almost forgotten not to trust him.

"Good," he said. "I want you to know the truth about me. I am no angel. Not even close. The Boha'a strive for balance, like all of the People. As for me, I've learned to embrace the darkness for protection. Outside of Abrani Daj I don't see much light in the people in my circle."

Camryn shivered as she wondered how much worse he could be than what she already experienced. Dagger always warned her not to trust him, not to think he was good at all. Why? Was it some type of manipulation on his part? Kind of a reverse psychology thing. Pretend to be honest so she would trust him, or was he truly telling her the truth?

She let out a breath she wasn't aware she was holding. No time to figure it out now. She needed to find her father.

"Do I even want to know what the tenth dimension is?" She asked.

Dagger smiled. "Traveling in the tenth dimension has never been accomplished by anyone in written history, but we know it is there. Here." He pointed to the last parchment. "Read the final text."

> *THE TENTH UNITES ALL*
> *Beware the Abaddon who seeks all there.*
> *The will of evil will strip the earth bare.*
> *Rise in song with sacred gateway trees*
> *And all of time will be freed for thee.*

"What is the Abaddon?" she asked.

"It is the compilation of all evil—all thoughts, all deeds, all those things that go against our duty to be compassionate with each other."

"Are you part of the Abaddon?" she asked in a whisper, afraid to hear the answer but needing to know what she faced.

"No," he said. "Darkness and evil are not one. Just as the light and good are not one."

She did not understand. Why was everything so confusing here? Where were the easy answers? She laughed and Dagger raised a brow in question.

"I'm looking for easy answers," she said. "I keep thinking how easy my life was before, but then I remember changing into everyone I saw wasn't exactly easy."

"And now?"

She looked up to the top of the tent, as if the answer was there. "And now the changes aren't happening. I don't know why, but it is a relief."

"The lichen controls them," he said.

"Figures. The one thing I really hate is that whole lichen thing and it's the only thing that's kept me sane."

He smiled. "You are very special, Camryn."

"Yeah, right. That's your come on line. Well it won't work."

He chuckled. "This time it isn't a line. But thanks for the tip not to use it in the future.

He pulled his chair closer to hers to face her directly. "Our prophecies tell us that the only forest person who can stop the Abaddon and become a tenth-dimensional being is a true Chameleon. A Chameleon who can change from one being to another is the only one with the ability to also become all things in the forest at once."

Camryn jumped from her seat and put both hands in front of her to make sure he came no closer. "Oh no. No, no, no, no, no. You are not going to lay that on me."

"I am only telling you of the prophecy. I'm not saying it's true and I'm not saying it's you."

"Right." She paced again. "And I have a choice. It's not me. Definitely not me. I have a whole boatload of problems already. I don't need to be thinking about being some unhuman, spiritual, tenth dimension freak." She paced faster. "Crap. Crap.

Crap. Why did you tell me that? Now, I won't get it out of my head. Now I'll have nightmares." She headed toward the front of the tent and pulled the entry flap aside.

"Where are you going?" Dagger asked.

She stopped but did not turn around. "Out. Away. I don't know."

"Running away?"

"No!" She paused. "Okay, maybe. I just can't handle this right now."

She felt a slight touch on her arm and slowly turned back toward him.

"You're tired, you're confused. It's understandable. Come back. You can sleep here and I'll help you get to your father tomorrow."

Camryn's gaze immediately went to the bed in the back of the tent. She could feel her cheeks getting red. "I don't think so. Absolutely not."

"I will not force the balvan ceremony on you."

"You've got that right, because I will not be spending the night."

"You have nowhere else to go tonight. The expectation is that you will be staying with me. No one else in the camp will invite you in. It is against the rules once you have completed the Kintala and a man has seen you and spent time with you."

"Well isn't that just convenient for you. Well forget it. I'll just find a place in the trees then. I've done it before. I'll do it again. I'll go back to the Alder."

"Are you willing to let the tree take you back to the Kintala visions? Are you willing to give yourself to the lichen tonight?"

She hadn't thought about that. But staying here with Dagger was worse. Wasn't it? She couldn't trust him. More than that, she couldn't trust herself with him. Now that she'd seen that aura thing, she wondered what other secret powers he might have or might be using on her already.

"Will it help if I sleep far away from you? You can have the bed and I'll sleep near the door."

There was absolutely no way she was getting into his bed, even without him. Having his smell so close would drive her crazy. "If you can promise you won't molest me, I'll stay," she said. "But I'll be the one sleeping near the door."

Dagger shrugged. "Have it your way." He pulled the two quilts off the camp chairs. "These should keep you pretty comfortable. Especially, with the fur tunic you're already wearing."

"Thanks." She took them and immediately placed them to one side of the tent flap to make up a bed on the floor.

When she stood again, he was within inches of her with a pillow from his bed. He lowered it at the end of the quilts farthest from the door. She couldn't move. She couldn't think. She couldn't talk.

He bent his head and his lips softly grazed hers. "Good night, Camryn."

As she crawled into her makeshift bed all she could think about was the feel of his lips, the warmth of his touch, and how much she now wished she were in that nice comfortable warm bed right next to him. The problem was she didn't know if that feeling was real, or if he'd magically done something to make her feel it, or if she was still suffering from parts of the Kintala.

She punched her pillow. Crap! Where was Ohar when she needed him? At least he made her feel safe. Well, except for that horrible dream. And except for the fact he was in love with Lyra but was directed to marry Camryn. She rolled onto her side and faced Dagger's bed. No one could be trusted. Not Ohar. Not Dagger. She had to remember that. Trust no one.

TRUST THE LICHEN

"This footwear does not look warm." He pointed to her black boots. The same ones she had been wearing since her escape from Starlight Center.

"They've been okay so far, " she said, looking down to where his hand lay upon her foot.

She'd woken at first light and Dagger was not in the tent. Before she could even get up and find a toilet he had returned with a breakfast of ham and eggs and warm blueberry muffins. She hurried toward the toilet in the camp and returned somewhat refreshed. They hadn't spoken much while eating. All she wanted was to get started finding her father, and it seemed all he wanted was to stop her from leaving.

Dagger stood and strode back to the trunk where he'd found the fur bands. "Take them off. They won't hold up in snow."

"Snow?" She swallowed the word, barely getting it out. "There's no snow around here."

He took out more bands of fur and leather. "I will tie your

feet in these and make a type of moccasin." He pushed her toward a camp chair. "Sit."

She sat awkwardly and he immediately took her left foot and began wrapping furs and molding the skin to her foot while securing it with the leather. He worked from her foot to her ankle, securing the new wrappings to the leggings he'd fashioned before.

"I told you, where you are going it's very cold."

"Yeah, but, how can I—"

"And I cannot go with you without putting you in even more danger." He finished quickly and lifted the other foot. This time his hands moved with even quicker speed to encase her right foot with fur and leather. "Now stand and let me make sure you can walk with this." He offered his hand to help her up.

Hesitant at first, and then with more confidence, Camryn made several circuits of the tent.

"They are quite comfortable and I don't think they'll fall off." She did a little twirl, feeling unlike herself. More free. More daring.

"Good. Now we go." He handed her the hat and the goggles.

She put the goggles on and laughed. "Really? I can barely see with these." She removed them and put them on her head.

"Camryn." Dagger reached for her head and stopped, looking at her face and into her eyes.

"I'm sorry," she said, unable to move, unable to think. "I'll wear them."

"Camryn." He put a little pressure to the back of her head and pulled it to his chest.

She snuggled there, wrapping her arms around his waist, wanting something, though she wasn't sure what she should want from him.

"I'm afraid for you," he finally said, his chest expanding and contracting beneath her cheek. "You aren't ready to do this alone." His hand caressed her back. "Perhaps you should wait. Stay here for a week, maybe two. Let me teach you more about the ways of the forest. Give yourself time to know your own power."

She sighed. How easy it would be to say yes. How hard it would be to not move forward now that she knew she had a purpose, a calling. Camryn raised her face to him. "I'll just have to learn along the way. Please, let's go now. Take me to the gateway tree before I change my mind."

His head dipped and he pressed his lips to hers. At first the light kiss asked permission, then he pressed firmly as she opened and let him in, his tongue seeking to know her most intimate secrets. She responded to his request with demands she had never planned to exercise with Dagger. She suddenly wanted to know all about him and why he made her feel this way.

His hands moved from her back to her head as he pulled her closer and deepened the kiss further. The world spun and stars sparkled in her mind. Moonlight and storm clouds fought overhead, each pulling her in different directions. She felt the initial dizziness, as if she would change into him, but she controlled it. Since the Kintala she rarely felt the pain anymore.

Camryn pushed against him until he finally released her. "I…" she stumbled against him, unbalanced.

He placed an arm firmly about her waist and held her close. "It's your Kintala calling to me," he said. "I felt it too."

Shortly the world stopped spinning and she was able to step back on her own.

"What did you say?"

"We are fated," he said.

Camryn shook her head of any vestiges of unbalance. "Wait just a darn minute. You said you didn't believe Arbani Daj and the whole first-male-to-see-me-after-the-Kintala thing."

"I don't. But I know what I felt just now."

"And that was?"

"Me responding to you."

"You mean sex. You were getting horny."

"Yes, that too. But it was more than that. The lichen chooses the match. There have been others among the Boha'a that have interested me sexually, but I've been waiting for my match. There has not been a true match until now."

Camryn held up her hand in that universal stop sign and shook her head. "Okay. Now you're acting too much like Ohar. He said I was already chosen for him by the Mazikeen. Now you say we are matched because of my Kintala and the whole lichen DNA thing."

"Ohar only wants power," Dagger ground out the words between his locked teeth and paced in front of her. "The mating he refers to is decreed by his mother, the Queen of the Mazikeen. It has nothing to do with fate or the lichen match. It has only to do with power."

With the kiss still fresh in her memory, Camryn wasn't sure of anything. Was it only yesterday she was sure Dagger would never be anything romantic to her? And now he was pairing them for life. What was it about the forest and the change—the Kintala—that made everything so crazy? If she could just get out of here and go home for a while, sneak back to her parent's home and just be alone, maybe she could sort out what was real and what was not. Had the forest, the lichen, placed a spell on her?

Camryn shook her head. She'd have to keep pushing through the confusion. First, she needed to find her father. He may have some answers that neither Ohar nor Dagger were willing to share.

"It's time for me to meet my father." She had to put any doubts behind her now.

Dagger nodded and offered his hand. "Running away won't make what I say false."

She crossed her arms across her chest. "Staying won't make it true."

Camryn followed him to the gateway tree. Neither of them chose to talk during the hike. She focused on her father, on the man named Nakani she had seen during her visions. She hoped Dagger really knew what he was doing and where he was sending her. If it was as cold as he said, she wouldn't have time to be trudging through the snow looking for him in miles of wasteland.

When they reached the gateway tree, she recognized it immediately. He gently placed her in front of it. She shivered in anticipation of the lichen suffocating her again. *Deep breaths,* she told herself and closed her eyes. *I can do this. Calm. Dagger said ask for it to enter.* She opened her eyes and stared straight at Dagger as she let out the first breath.

"Are you sure you want to go?"

Camryn nodded, though she wasn't sure at all.

"Remember. Welcome the lichen. Let it guide you."

She closed her eyes and took a deep breath in again and let it out. She would try to welcome it, but it was darn hard to ask furry green stuff to smother you.

"Remember. You must keep the eighth dimension in your head as you travel. Ask the lichen to take you to the Eighre Terrace. Think of your father—the name Nakani. Don't let your mind wander or think of anything else."

She nodded again. So many rules. She'd have to focus. The

last thing she wanted was to not find her father or to lose her way back. She closed her eyes again and breathed in, this time inviting the lichen to her. She chanted in her mind. *Eighth dimension. Eighre terrace. Nakani. Eighth dimension. Eighre terrace. Nakani.*

She gasped and her eyes opened wide when she felt the first tendrils wrap around her waist.

"Don't be afraid," Dagger repeated and pulled the goggles over her eyes. "It will warm you. The lichen will keep you safe."

She tried to believe him, but she couldn't help the panic as she felt her feet and then her legs become encased. Pressure on her shoulders forced her head back toward the tree, then her head locked to the trunk, paralyzing her. Only sensations in her face remained. She knew soon she would see nothing of Dagger. Nothing of the Boha'a camp. Nothing at all.

"Look at me, Camryn, and listen." Dagger kept his eyes locked on hers. "I don't have much time left before you are gone."

She tried to nod, but could no longer move her head.

"I am not certain which tree on the mountain the lichen will choose for you," Dagger said. "But when you step from the gateway tree, be careful. It will be snow and ice. You may be near a cliff and could easily step off. Don't move until you have your bearings. Don't move until you can see steps to take you down from the terrace."

"And where will I find my father?" she asked. Her voice the only thing she could exercise now. She felt as if her legs and arms were melting into the tree. Then her torso seemed to disappear. Only her face was still conscious.

"His prison is in an ice cave below the Eighre Terrace," Dagger said. "You will know it because it will be dug into the side of the ice, with unbreakable bars holding him there."

"How will I free him?"

He looked at her one last time and bent to kiss her. "I don't know," he said. "All I know is that you will find a way."

His lips seared hers with warmth and promise. When he moved back the lichen covered her face.

COLD TRUTH

Camryn's mind automatically reached into the forest networks eternal flow to pull out the Eighre Terrace location she needed. One by one the three chants—*Eighre Terrace, Eighth Dimension, Nakani*—grew into brilliance inside her mind, filling it until she could think of nothing else. She drew the knowledge into her mouth and the lichen filled her lungs. Her body felt like a whirling ball of frosted breath that grew until it was an arm's span wide. It drifted through a network of trees and stars and lichen and forest duff. Then, its work done, the ball of her consciousness was taken by the wind and breathed out of a tree, and her body resolved onto a terrace of snow and ice.

Camryn squinted, her sight obscured by frosted goggles and the snow that covered nearly all her face. Some whistled notes, redolent with power, drifted up to Camryn, and for a nausea-inducing moment she felt as if she were flying and being tossed in the wind.

Then there was nothing but silence and white snow and ice everywhere. Suddenly, the sky darkened and there came a great noise, and flashes of lightning cut the darkness. A deep whirring sound, like giant wings beating, came from above her. She turned to gaze toward the sky and a huge, bird-shaped creature with a long tail and flashing kaleidoscope eyes resolved out of the clouds. This bird was larger than any she'd ever seen. Its head was…oh god, it was the head of a dragon, and its eyes glowed like fire, but it's wings were feathers, not scales. When the dragon-bird flapped its wings, thunder sounded and the winds increased and lightning followed whenever it opened and shut its eyes.

The feathered wings swooped down, turned into the wind, and came to a sliding, snow-spraying stop on the terrace perhaps fifty feet from where she clung to the tree. A fur-bundled person was atop its back. The person looked in her direction and she scooted behind the trunk of the tree.

Please, please don't come this direction. I'm not here. I'm not here. She closed her eyes as if not looking would ensure the person would not investigate.

The dragon roared and she opened her eyes and peered around the tree trunk. Urged by the person riding it, the dragon dove off the cliff to what she assumed was a landing site well below.

The clouds immediately cleared, and cold and sunshine hit her at the same time, the former strong enough to feel even through her heavy clothes, and the latter fierce enough to make her half-close her eyes, even behind goggles. Though the sky appeared cloudless and full of summer sunshine, it was freezing on the snowy terrace. The chill came from the breeze that blew along the terrace and then up, over, and around the mountain.

Ahead of Camryn, a broad, unnaturally flat glacier had carved a terrace into the mountainside. Snow and chunks of ice piled all around the edges in deep drifts. On the far side of the terrace, the mountain fell away in a sheer precipice. Camryn looked across it, hoping to see where the dragon and rider had landed, but she saw nothing but blue sky and a few wisps of low clouds.

She shivered and looked away. She wondered if she was crazy to attempt this. She forced herself to move and take a few steps across the terrace, to at least take a look at the drop. What if she slipped and went over the edge to her death? What if the dragon and rider weren't exactly happy to see her? What in the world made her think she was brave enough to do this?

She headed back to the gateway tree, having walked the length of the terrace four times without once daring to go anywhere near the cliff to look for a way down. The closest she'd managed was three or four feet from the sudden drop at the end of the terrace, where she'd verified the dragon and its rider were indeed on a second, smaller outcrop about thirty feet below. But she saw no way down to investigate. No stairs like Dagger had mentioned and no evidence of a cave with bars holding her father.

Camryn heard the deep rumble of thunder again. Lightning followed as she looked up to the darkening sky and a second dragon-like bird appeared out of the dark clouds. This one was imbued with many shades of blue and aimed straight at her. She looked back at the approaching dragon, then at the precipice, her head moving in frantic starts. She ran for the gateway tree.

The dragon's wings clipped the top of the tree where she cowered. It made two circles, each time roaring as if it knew she was there. She could barely make out a person covered in furs similar to the ones she wore, with reins in his or her hands pulling the bird toward the precipice. As the blue feathers spread to slow the descent, the dragon and rider dropped out of sight.

Camryn scrambled to the edge again to see if the two dragon-birds were now united. The white one was still below with its rider pacing nearby, but she could not see the blue one anywhere. She turned to search the sky and screamed in terror.

Large talons contracted around her waist. Her scream was silenced in the rush of wind pummeling her small form as blue wings flapped around her and hoisted her into the sky. Camryn curled in tight to strengthen her hold on the bird's feet. She felt like a quivering ball of fur and goggles as the-bird dropped over the edge and the ground rushed toward her.

Camryn squeezed her eyes closed, certain of her impending death when she inevitably crashed into the snow. Then the talons opened and released her from its grip. Her heart stalled and her eyes snapped open. She fell only a few feet to a cushion of powdered snow plowed in front of where the white dragon rested.

"Wynbune? What are you doing here? How did you get here?"

Camryn uncurled at the sound of Ohar's voice, though she still couldn't recognize him behind the snow covered furs he wore from head to toe.

The rider on the blue dragon stepped forward and wrapped her arms around Camryn. "I'm so sorry, Camryn," a familiar female voice sounded near her ear. "I didn't realize it was you when I commanded my thunder dragon to pick you up. I was afraid you were a spy for the Agnoses."

Camryn pushed away from the embrace. "A spy? Why would they want to spy on anyone? Who are you?" She turned back to

Ohar. "What are you doing here? Is it your intent to imprison me like my father."

"Wynbune, I would never—"

The female unwrapped her face and Camryn recognized her immediately. "Sela?" She looked from Ohar to Sela. "I don't understand. You're...you're..."

Sela shook her head. "No, I'm not Mazikeen. I have no powers. I am an Agnoses watcher for the Forest People."

Camryn again shifted her gaze from Ohar to Sela. It was crazy enough to realize dragons even existed. But given what she'd experienced so far in the forest it wasn't a stretch that one more myth would prove true.

"Agnoses can ride dragons?" she asked, hoping that most people—people like Dr. Frenelli—didn't even know about dragons.

"I don't know," Sela answered. "I don't know any other Agnoses who travel the forest network except me. Though I've heard there are a few in other places in the world. I am very fortunate. At an early age I knew about the Forest People, but I waited too long to make my choice to join them. Though I cannot travel the tree network, the forest has provided many other things for me. And the Mazikeen appointed me your protector in the Agnoses world.

"When I was chosen to be your protector, Ohar's mother took me to Arach Falls for a choosing. We didn't know if I would be chosen, but we hoped a thunder dragon would bond with me. It makes it significantly easier for me to travel to the different tribes. I knew the choosing was successful when my thunder dragon—my Adalinda—greeted me by saying 'Protector of the Chameleon, Welcome.'" Sela's eyes misted and she swallowed.

"They talk?" Camryn asked.

"Yes," Sela said. "Actually, it's not aloud, it's in your mind."

Camryn tried to imagine being chosen by a dragon. Was it like having a pet? A dog or cat, but bigger. No, she couldn't imagine it. And she definitely couldn't imagine any animal speaking to her through some type of telepathy.

"Do you know where my father is?" she asked Sela.

Sela stepped forward and cocked her head to one side. "Camryn, you know your father is dead. Your mother and father died in a car crash. That was how you ended up at Starlight Center."

"Yes, my adoptive parents are dead. But I've now learned of my biological parents and that the Mazikeen have imprisoned my father somewhere in this area."

Camryn turned to Ohar. "You know where he is. Tell me. I want to see him."

"What is this, Ohar? Is this true?" Sela asked, her voice stern.

Ohar sighed. "It's not what it seems."

"What do you mean?" Sela said. "Either you have imprisoned her father or not. Which is it?"

Camryn turned to Sela. "They sent my father to prison for murder because my mother died while giving birth to me and they hold him responsible. He is imprisoned because he loved my mother, a Mazikeen and he is a Quatcho, and that is not allowed." She turned to Ohar.

Tears stung Camryn's eyes. "The love my parents had for each other was real. They both knew what would happen if she became pregnant. They both chose anyway."

"He knew the rules. He chose his fate." Ohar splayed his hands out to the side. "Things are different in our world. We run things differently, more justly than the Agnoses world where you grew up. It is required for us to survive. This is not for you to decide, Wynbune."

"I don't care about your stupid rules," Camryn yelled. "Love is not something to be punished."

"It's the murder we punish," Ohar said.

"It's not my father's fault my mother died. They chose together. It's as much my mother's fault as his."

"Yes, and she is dead. She suffered the consequences of her decision. Now your father must suffer the consequences as well. He is a murderer by Mazikeen law."

"Tell me where he is." Camryn pushed at his chest.

"No. I can't."

"Can't? Or won't?"

Ohar shrugged.

"Dagger was right. You don't truly care for me. You don't care if your stupid laws are right or wrong. What is it you really want, Ohar? What game are you playing?"

"Oh, so you believe the Boha'a thief now? The one who kidnapped you?"

"I believe him in this. At least he is honest with me about his agenda. That's more than I can say for you. You can't even stand up for yourself against your mother. You can't even stand up for the woman you loved. Lyra!"

Ohar's eyes widened and his nostrils flared, but he said nothing. He stood stiff and still.

After a moment of the two of them staring in a standoff, Ohar clenched his teeth together. "You know nothing of my love for Lyra. And you will not speak of it again."

Camryn looked away. He was right. It was a low blow. She kind of felt sorry for Ohar. His mother must be a real witch, forcing him to marry someone he didn't love.

"Either you help me find my father or you lose my trust forever. If you refuse me, whatever scheme you have about me and you and the Mazikeen is ruined. I will refuse to go anywhere with you. You can imprison me and I still won't do anything you ask."

"Wynbune—"

"And my name is Camryn." She stomped her foot in the snow. "That is the one piece of my identity I know for sure, and you always try to take it away—to brainwash me—every time you don't use my name. Well, it won't work." She turned and walked past him, marching toward the cliff face.

"Wyn…Camryn, where are you going?" Ohar shouted at her retreating back.

She stopped and whipped back around. "If you won't help me, I'll look for him myself, and you can't stop me." She turned back and continued her journey.

"You won't find him here." Ohar yelled into the wind.

Camryn didn't respond. She kept walking toward the face of snow and ice. She didn't know how she would scale it. And even if she found a way up, she had no idea where to begin to search for her father.

She was tired of being buffeted between competing agendas. She was tired of not knowing the whole truth about her parents, her gifts and how to use them, her purpose in being here. She was tired of both Ohar and Dagger thinking they had some right to her heart and her body. As she couldn't trust anyone to tell her the truth, she'd have to seek it on her own.

"Wait!" Camryn turned at Sela's voice. "You can't go off alone." Sela caught up and stopped a couple of feet from Camryn. A hesitant smile turned her lips up slightly, reminding her of all the times Sela had calmed her at Starlight Center, all the little things she had done to befriend Camryn and to make the days not as terrible.

"I'm sure you have questions," Sela said. "I'm sure you

wonder about my part in this, and you are right not to trust me any more than Ohar. But please know that everything I have done was to keep you safe. Everything I have done is to help not only the Mazikeen, but also the Boha'a, and the Quatcho, and the many Forest People you don't even know exist."

Camryn wanted to believe her, but this was yet one more person who had evidently known things about her and had chosen to keep silent. She stiffened her spine and lifted her chin. She put all her distrust into her stare back to Sela. "Do you know where my father is?"

Sela shook her head. "No, but we have a better chance of finding him together than you going off on your own."

"I don't trust you."

"I don't blame you," Sela said. "You trusted me once. I would like the chance to earn it again."

She reached toward Camryn and Camryn took a step back. "Why didn't you tell me about my past when I was at Starlight Center? Why didn't you tell me about the forest and what I would find? The Kintala? My gifts? Why?"

Sela sighed and lowered her eyes. "Because of you."

"Me? If you knew who I was, my background, my so-called gifts and how the puzzle fits together, why didn't you tell me before? Why didn't you tell me to leave Starlight Center?"

Camryn stared hard at Sela, daring her to lie. Daring her to come up with a meaningless excuse. She wasn't sure whom to trust anymore. It seemed everyone knew a lot more about her and her life than she did. And no one was willing to tell her the whole truth.

"Things are much more complicated with you," Sela said.

"Yeah, tell me about it. I'm the first Chameleon in more than a thousand years. That's darn complicated enough."

"I'm trying to protect you."

"What do you really want from me?"

Sela reached to take Camryn's hands, but Camryn crossed them in front of her, tucked them under her arms.

"Truly, I didn't know your father still lived. I thought both your father and mother had died and that was one of the reasons you were adopted into an Agnoses family.

"The Starlight Center is also not to be trusted. Anyone with abilities beyond the norm is taken to Starlight Center for study. Dr. Frenelli has some type of special contract with the government that I don't understand. We have found Forest People trapped there. I'm not sure how. When I learned *you* had been sent there, I knew I had to get a job as your nurse and make sure you were protected."

"People trapped? Why? What are they doing?" Camryn began to shake as memories of drugs and hallucinations came back to her.

"I don't know what the research does," Sela said. "All I know is it somehow enhances powers."

"Dr. Frenelli knows I have powers? Magical powers?"

"Yes, I'm sure he does."

Camryn paced back and forth. This was bad. This meant even Frenelli knew something about her she didn't know. Everyone wanted a piece of her.

"There are also many groups in the forest who would harm you. Tribes taken over by the Abaddon—the darkness—who would have killed you as a baby if they could. Now that you are among the People, you will have enemies following you, looking for a chance to destroy you."

"Why? What have I done to any of them?"

"You exist," Sela said. "No one knows how much your

powers will grow. We already know you are the most powerful of any of the Forest People."

"I didn't ask for any of this. I don't want it. All I ever wanted was to be normal. To find one identity and hang on to it. To live a normal life like any other teenager. I want to go to college, to have a career, to find a boyfriend. I don't want any powers."

Sela gathered Camryn into her chest. "I know this must be horribly confusing for you."

Camryn struggled to hold back the tears. She felt comfortable once again in Sela's embrace. For the first time since escaping Starlight Center, she felt like someone actually cared about her instead of some broader agenda. She mumbled into Sela's chest, "I'm not the prophecy."

Sela patted her back "It is one part of who you are, Camryn. It is as much a part of your identity as your Mazikeen mother and Quatcho father."

Camryn stepped away from Sela's embrace and gathered her emotions, stuffing them again in a lockbox in her mind. She swallowed and looked up.

"I'm sorry I didn't help you more at Starlight Center," Sela said. "By the time I found you there and became one of your nurses, Dr. Frenelli already had already sold the information to a secret physiology team to use your DNA in some experiment. He was making arrangements to have you moved. I knew you had to escape, but I didn't know how to make that happen. That's why I sent Ohar to you."

"You did?" Camryn looked to Ohar. "Sela asked you to come?"

Ohar stepped closer. "Yes. We thought we had lost you forever."

"Ohar was the only one of the Mazikeen who could spend more than twenty-four hours in the Agnoses world," Sela said.

Camryn took a step back from both Ohar and Sela. "I can't trust him."

Sela bit her bottom lip. "He is a Mazikeen and beholding to the Queen. But he is a good man. He saved me from a Vrag. That's how he got his pendant."

Ohar advanced on Sela, his eyes wide and deep breaths puffing his chest out. "And that is why you should have trusted me and the Mazikeen completely. Was it this non-trust that kept you from letting the Mazikeen know about Wyn…Camryn being trapped in Starlight Center sooner?"

"It's not just you, Ohar." Sela stood her ground, unflinching. "It's all of the Mazikeen, and the Boha'a and the Quatcho and any other group that has designs on controlling Camryn."

Ohar stood only a foot away from Sela and stared her down. "How dare you! You are Agnoses and you dare to question the divine path of the lichen? The path chosen for the Chameleon?"

"That's right." Sela stood nose to nose with him. "I dare because I seem to be the only one who has Camryn's best interests at heart. I am the only one who cares that all the forest people are saved, not just one group who will rule the others."

Camryn stepped between them and pushed them apart. "Where is my father?"

Ohar took a deep breath and let it out slowly, as if it was a struggle for him to calm himself. Camryn waited until she saw his shoulders lower. "Where is he?"

"He is no longer here. He's been moved."

"Where?"

"I can't tell you."

"Can't or won't?"

Ohar shrugged.

Camryn raised her chin. "Fine. I'll look for him on my own until I find him. I'm not completely helpless anymore. At least I have Dagger, and I have the tree network. I'll learn whatever I need to enhance my powers in order to find my father."

"You won't survive alone. You need me."

"Then I'll be dead and your prophecy will be dead too. So everyone loses."

Camryn crossed her arms with confidence and stared him down.

"Ventiat Glacier." Ohar said it as if it were forced from him.

"Thank you."

She turned to Sela and pulled her back to the other side of the glacier where the two dragons lounged. Camryn reached and stoked its side. The dragon snorted, but it wasn't too scary.

"Her name is Adalinda," Sela said. "She's a thunder dragon."

"Thunder dragon, huh? I've never heard of that."

"As with everything among the Forest People, it's a mutation from the lichen."

Ohar pulled himself up on his thunder dragon and secured straps around his wrists. "According to our ancient texts, thousands of years ago giant dragon lizards were gifted with the Thunder Bird spirit and the knowledge of the world from its beginning. That is why they are called Thunder Dragons. Their heads and tails resemble that of the dragon lizards, but their core—their heart—is from the Thunder Bird. Only bonded riders can fly."

Ohar's dragon wings beat heavily and it ascended into the sky. Camryn couldn't see it for long. When it reached the clouds it was like it disappeared.

"Riding a dragon sounds pretty cool." Camryn stroked Adalinda's side again.

The dragon sniffed her and snorted. Camryn ran her fingers through the soft, downy blue feathers and smiled. Then just as she saw Ohar do, she used the straps to pull her astride Adalinda.

"Wait!" Sela shouted.

"Aren't you going to teach me to fly?"

"I'll do better than that. I'll help you find your own thunder dragon."

RESCUE

amryn stood at the first ice shelf, her hand shielding her eyes from the sun's glare as she scanned the sky for Sela and Dagger on their thunder dragons. Koška and her mate, Mykah, had joined Camryn traveling the network to the gateway tree six miles from the west end of Ventiat Glacier. Though she wasn't cold, Camryn shivered beneath her layers of fur as she scanned the distance they had trudged for the past several hours.

The glacier chiseled a swath of ice-filled valley thirty to forty miles long between five major ridges on the north, south, and east. The mountains directed freezing winds along the trough. With temperatures on the valley floor never above freezing, Camryn was glad it was summer now. Though Koška and Mykah could have shifted to their cat form and easily run over the snow and ice, they chose to accompany Camryn and make sure she didn't fall or slip into danger.

During the trek, Koška and Mykah had told the story of a

place at Ventiat Glacier that Mazi-Chatul universally feared. It was called Kishuf Ke'rach—Magic Ice. It is said that when the lichen mutated some Mazikeen into cat-shifters thousands of years ago, the chambers behind the frozen waterfall were used to imprison them—hoping to starve the cat-shifters into extinction and break the mutated lichen DNA within them. The spell the Mazikeen queen had cast upon the icefall caused it to move every day at unpredictable times and in unpredictable patterns so that the shifters would never escape and no Mazikeen sympathizers would find them. If there were an ice prison at the Ventiat Glacier, Mykah believed Kishuf Ke'rach was it and that it began where they stood now.

The skies darkened and lightning danced above them. Camryn looked up and heard the thunder signaling Dagger and Sela's arrival. The two thunder dragons easily landed in front of her and formed a shield against the wind at the base of Kishuf Ke'rach.

The band of five together wandered toward the edge of the icefall. A series of ladders and ropes were strung along its surface suggesting that someone used them to traverse this area on a regular basis. Camryn shielded her eyes against the blinding sunlight as she looked up the fall and across the jigsaw puzzle of giant white ice pieces poised on the edge of deep blue crevasses that could easily kill someone who slipped while climbing. The thin, ice-edged cracks appeared to drop hundreds of feet from the top to even below where she stood. Because of the height of the fall, she couldn't see how long or wide they might get. From her vantage point below she could tell that some crevasses were loosely covered in snow in several places, creating a death trap for the unwary climber. She found it hard to imagine how they would all hopscotch uphill through a field of ice boulders the size of houses that could shift at any moment without warning and plunge them to their death. Camryn crossed her arms tightly in front of her.

Dagger moved to stand directly in her line of sight but did not touch her. "We *will* find your father."

She worried her lower lip. "How can you be sure?" She swallowed. "How could anyone survive here? I couldn't bear it to come so far and find him frozen dead."

"The Quatcho are covered in fur that thickens in winter. He would not die from cold."

"Then starvation," Camryn said. "Mykah told us the Mazikeen intended to starve the cat-shifters here. Why would they choose to keep my father alive?"

"Because of you. Because they need you. Perhaps, if you had undergone the Kintala with them and been immediately mated with Ohar…"

Camryn looked away.

"I'm sorry.' He reached for her and she sidestepped his touch. "I didn't mean to suggest—"

She took a step backward to increase the distance.

"What I meant to say was if you had agreed to marry Ohar then the Mazikeen would have let your father die. They would have had what they wanted."

"Or perhaps they would have let him out of prison, as a present to me," Camryn countered. "Why do you always think the worst of them?"

Dagger clenched his hands at his side. "Old habits. Perhaps you are right. Perhaps they would have finally let him go for your nuptials."

"I can see you don't believe that."

"I'm trying, Camryn. That's all I can do. You cannot ask me

to change everything I know, everything I am, and believe the Mazikeen to be filled with light."

Camryn looked past him to the giant icefall behind. "When you kidnapped me and I underwent the Kintala with the Boha'a, did you fear they would kill my father?"

"No. I knew they would need him more than ever. I knew they would use him as a bargaining chip to get your cooperation."

She stepped forward to within inches of him and looked up to his face, determined to show she was not afraid of him or his words. "Is that why you took me? To save my father?"

Dagger's cheeks pulled in and he stared at her hard. "Do not think that I am a good man, Camryn. If I took you to save your father, it was not out of altruism. It was only to get back at the Mazikeen. It was only to use you as a bargaining chip for lifting the Fordun curse from the Boha'a."

"And now?" She held his stare with equal ferocity. "Do you still plan to use me as a bargaining chip?"

"No," he whispered. "No."

In spite of her promises not to fall under his spell, not to trust anyone, she couldn't help but hang onto the hope Dagger offered. Hope that her father was indeed still alive."

A cat's roar startled Camryn and she turned toward the sound, her arms close to her side, her fists ready for an attack. Nine cats circling the five of them.

Dagger sidled next to her, and Sela quietly edged closer.

"Where did they all come from?" Sela whispered.

"I don't know," Dagger said. "But they are all shifters."

"Do all fae-shifters get along?" Camryn asked.

"I don't know. I've never seen these colorings before. I don't know where they live. They are not part of the Mazikeen shifters I know."

Koška and Mykah shifted to their cat forms and reared on their hind legs in a protective stance. The nine shifted at once to their fae bodies. Three males, six females. Mykah and Koška followed suit returning to fae as well.

"Which is the Chameleon?" the largest male asked.

Dagger stepped in front of Sela and Camryn, his arms pushing them both well behind him.

Koška breached the protective circle and walked toward the other fae. "It's okay. I believe they have been helping Nakani. I believe they want to know that his daughter truly lives."

Camryn stepped forward.

"No," Dagger grabbed her arm. "It might be a trick."

She looked at him and removed his hand. "I trust Koška. You should too."

His eyes widened in surprise. Then he dropped his head and stepped back.

"I am the Chameleon," Camryn said with as much confidence as she could muster. "Who asks for me?"

The large male stepped to her, his body bare except for a piece of leather around his waist that reached to just above his knees. He towered over her by a good foot and a half. "How do I know you tell the truth?"

Camryn smiled, looked at him and then concentrated on controlling her change. She did not scream out when she felt her head enlarge, her legs and torso stretch as her breasts retracted and the furs she wore slipped to the ground. She did not let anyone know of the pain that coursed through her nerve endings as muscle grew and filled in her legs and arms, as her feet outgrew her boots and changed to be large and flat with hair tufts on the bottom and between the toes. When she had finally become the man who stood in front of her, the rest of his tribe were on one knee staring up at her and mumbling. "The prophecy is true. The Quatcho was telling the truth. The Chameleon has come to save us."

In the voice of the man who had questioned her, Camryn said. "I am the Chameleon. Take me to my father, the Quatcho Nakani imprisoned here."

Camryn returned to herself and the Mazi-chatuls led them all through a maze of crevasses and hidden passages beneath Kishuf Ke'rach. As they moved deeper into the abyss of light and shadow, Camryn realized she never would have found her father without them.

Only a thin blue line divided fantasy from geology in the labyrinth of passageways they followed. Ice spires threatened to impale anyone who fell from the narrow path. Amid the frozen walls and sheer drops of raw edged stone, fantastically animated forms shimmered in shades of blues, purples, and creams, adding to her confusion with each new twist and turn in the path.

During the journey, they learned that the Mazikeen had in fact left Nakani to die. But these shifters were the ancestors of the original Mazi-chatuls imprisoned here previously. The original shifters had escaped their prison by friends bringing fire starters and melting the bars over several years of attempts. It was then that the Mazikeen created the ice-moving spell and rebuilt the bars every night.

The freed shifters made their homes in ice caves several miles away. They vowed to learn the movements each night and to find a way to overcome the spell should their kind ever be imprisoned again. Only Nakani had been brought there in the lives of the current pride. Though they could not help him escape, they provided a constant supply of food and kept him company as he awaited the return of his daughter.

"Prepare yourself, the final drop is the most dangerous," the Mazi-chatul leader said to Camryn. "The prison is near. Do not fear. Your father is well."

The final drop descended over one thousand feet in sixteen, crazy-steep, zigzagging switchbacks, like a spiral staircase carved right into the huge block of ice. Over hundreds of years, the Mazi-chatul had maintained a series of chained handholds to grab and hang onto as the path often tipped at a sharp angle.

Suddenly, the tight turns ended, and the tunnel of blue ice opened into a large ice cave more than three stories tall and a block wide. It was dissected by round ice bars, reaching from ceiling to floor, each at least four feet wide and spaced five or six inches apart. Behind the bars a Quatcho waited. Over seven feet tall, thick hair covering him from head to foot, his eyes tracked her approach.

Camryn ran forward. "Father!" Her arms reached between the bars to touch him as tears coursed down her face. "You live. You live."

Without thinking, she turned into a small Quatcho girl. Her own body quickly sprouting hair matching the coloring of her father.

"Wynbune, I knew you would come." Nakani stroked her head as best he could through the bars. "At long last I see you again."

It was several minutes before either one could speak again.

"You honor me with your Quatcho self," Nakani said. "But I beg you to return to your true self," Nakani said. "I wish to see you as the daughter of my Fia."

Camryn easily switched to the visage of her mother, Fia, as she remembered from her Kintala dreams.

Nakani froze. His hand clutched hers tightly and she could

feel the acceleration of his heartbeat. His throat distended with swallow after swallow.

After a full minute he finally whispered, "It is my true love. The one I lost so long ago." He rubbed at his eyes with his other hand. "I have held your mother forever in my heart. I thank you for this blessing, but it is you, I wish to see, Wynbune. The true you."

"Oh father," Camryn cried out in Fia's voice. "But I do not know the true me. I have not seen her. I have not felt her. I don't know how to find her."

Nakani took her face between his large hands on either side of the bars and held it steady. "Look at me, Wynbune."

She opened her eyes wide, though they were filled with tears.

"You approached me as your true self. Do you not know that? It was the child in my dreams. The babe who had become a beautiful young woman. You are yourself when you do not try to be someone else. You are yourself when you sleep, when you dream, when you act in good faith. Do you not know that girl?"

Camryn shook her head in confusion.

"Ask your friends. They have surely seen the true you."

She grasped her father's hand and turned to Sela and Dagger and Koška. "Have you seen my true self?"

They all nodded.

"Describe her to me."

"You are a girl of great courage and honesty," Sela said.

"You are one who trusts easily, even when you think you shouldn't," Koška offered.

"You are light and shadow in balance. You are at once innocence and guilt. You are incorruptible and I …." Dagger stopped midsentence, his chest rising and falling as he stepped closer.

"Look inside, Camryn. You have accepted that you are the Chameleon. Now accept that you are Wynbune and Camryn and you will see from within your true self."

She shook her head and sank to the ground. "You are not telling me what I look like. How can I change to be that girl? How can I always look the same so that others will recognize me?"

"But we do recognize you," Dagger said sitting next to her. "Your father is right. When you sleep, when you take action, when you walk in the forest next to me without concentrating on being someone else I only see the true you. Look closely and you will see her too."

Camryn closed her eyes and searched for this girl everyone knew but herself. Tears leaked beneath her lashes and she couldn't catch her breath. Her father stroked her head from the other side of his prison. Dagger held her hand, his thumb tracing calming circles along her knuckles. She concentrated inward, like she did when she was stuck in the Zwischen. She concentrated like she did when she healed Koška. She opened her heart to finally see herself.

She smiled at the girl before her. Her height and weight were unchanged from the girl she had chosen to be just before leaving Starlight Center, but her hair was shorter. Instead of almost waist length, it was cropped close to her face and her neckline. Brown with streaks of golden starlight. Her face was like her mother, Fia, but with a slightly stronger nose and wider lips like her father.

This was the girl born Wynbune of a Mazikeen mother and a Quatcho father. Wynbune, the faerie name for Chameleon. Raised in the Agnoses world by her wonderful adopted parents as Camryn. All along her true self had been there, safe inside, waiting for her to embrace it instead of running from it. Finally she knew her true self. Finally she had an identity. Finally she saw what her friends had seen all along, the integration of Wynbune and Camryn. She was all of them and she was one unique individual as the Chameleon.

Camryn stood and faced the cold ice bars, her knowledge of herself infused confidence in the powers she held inside. "It is time for you to be released, father."

"I have been released," Nakani replied. "By seeing you I have been released from my internal prison."

"Stand back," Camryn said. "I don't know what will happen." She turned to those who stood behind her. "Everyone, stand far away. I'm not always in control. I don't want anyone to get hurt."

Nakani covered her small hand at the ice bar with his furry one. "I don't want you hurt. I am satisfied to stay here. I have the Mazi-chatul to bring me food and company. Please, Wynbune. Please do not hurt yourself for me."

"I'm going to do this if you are near or far. I can't stand the thought of you spending another night imprisoned in here. So, please move away so I can concentrate better."

Nakani stepped a few feet back. He would go no further.

Camryn looked behind her. The others had been more cautious. They were at least twenty feet away, almost to the passageway to exit the cavern.

Camryn closed her eyes and placed her hands out to her sides. She called on the sun above to join with the lichen within her and give her strength. She called on the heat from below to send its warmth into the cavern. The bars shimmered and began to melt. The floor below steamed as water dropped from the bars and met the uprising of ancient volcanic lava. Sweat beaded along her brow and trickled down her neck as she concentrated even harder.

"Camryn!' Dagger shouted. "Stop! Pull back! It's too much. The whole thing will collapse!"

She opened her eyes and heard the screams as the Mazichatul all shifted to cats at once and ran from her down the passageway.

"Sela, go!" Dagger shouted. "I'll get her. Run!"

Sela turned and followed the cats as quickly as she could.

Camryn tried to pull back the energy. She tried to think cooling thoughts, to pull forth the power of the snows of the glacier, but it was too late. Geysers erupted all around her. The bars were still standing, but not for long. She feared the ceiling would cave before her father got through.

"Father! Hurry!" she yelled. "I can't stop it." She pushed at the bars, hoping to break one or two for him to get through.

"Stand back," Nakani yelled as the rumble of an earthquake below them caught Camryn off guard and she fell, hitting her head against the ice.

Nakani took a running start and broke through two of the weakened prison bars, at the same time scooping Camryn into his arms and running for the exit. "Dagger, show me the way out."

Dagger ran ahead, using his own energy to hold the tunnel passageway together. He was not adept at calling forth the elements of ice or cooling, but he had long known he could throw or hold heavy objects in stasis as a means of protection. With each turn Dagger chose, the tunnel collapsed behind Nakani as he concentrated on the passage in front of them. As the handholds broke apart, and the path fell, creating new fissures, Dagger quickly directed boulders and large blocks of ice to make a new path for them. At the same time he had to hold large blocks of falling ice above them as they ran, and lift others out of the way. He'd never worked so hard, so fast. His head pounded in pain with the effort.

When Dagger and Nakani finally exited to the outside, Dagger collapsed near his dragon, Qadir. His breath came in fits and starts. He could no longer hold anything together. The ground shook beneath them as another earthquake cracked a large fissure, separating them from Kishuf Ke'rach.

"Place her on Qadir," Dagger instructed Nakani between breaths.

"But she cannot ride with you," Nakani said. "It is death for you and Qadir."

She is the Chameleon, Qadir said in Dagger's mind. *She can ride with us. The thunder dragons will not abandon her now.*

"Qadir says it's safe," Dagger pointed to where Nakani should place her.

Nakani did as instructed and then turned to heft Dagger onto Qadir as well. He secured the straps around both Wynbune and Dagger and cinched them tight. "Go before it is too late!"

"How will you escape?" Dagger asked. "If I leave you to die after Wynbune has just found you, she will never forgive me."

"I will follow the tracks of the Mazi-chatul. They have been coming here to help me for the past decade. If they have escaped, I will as well."

Dagger sent out a plea to the powers of the earth and sky that the melting remain localized, that it would not endanger the shifters. "We will follow you as long as we can," he said to Nakani.

Nakani kissed Wynbune's unconscious head, then ran in giant loping leaps, his large frame easily jumping over boulders and fissures in his path. Dagger watched him follow the cat prints in the snow as they moved toward the frozen mountain peaks on the northern side of the glacier.

When he could no longer see Nakani, he finally allowed his eyes to close. He was exhausted and he didn't trust himself to stay awake for the journey. "Qadir please keep in contact with Adalinda and Sela. Shadow Nakani to make sure he is safe and finds shelter."

I am always in contact with my kind. We rise together. We protect together.

Qadir took a running start and easily rose into the sky, climbing at a gentle incline, then headed north across the great mountains to follow Nakani and the Mazul-chatul.

The Chameleon sleeps, but she is well. Qadir said. *Now you must sleep.*

Dagger patted Qadir's neck. "Thank you for monitoring her."

Kishuf Ke'rach has collapsed inward into the cavern.

"How do you know?" Dagger knew that thunder dragons had a special communication with each other, but he had seen no other dragons except Adalinda near the icefall.

The earth reports the geyser warmth has stopped. It healed the fissures and they have refrozen solid. There are no longer passages beneath the fall.

"Then the prison is gone?" Dagger asked.

The place you found the Quatcho no longer exists.

"What does that mean?"

The Chameleon took the Mazikeen magic from it. It no longer exists in any dimensional space.

Dagger let go a low whistle of appreciation. No wonder Camryn was exhausted. She probably had no idea what she had done. If she ever learned to control her power, maybe the prophecy would come true. Maybe she really could defeat the Abaddon and find the cure to the lichen mutations.

Dagger wrapped an arm about her waist and pulled her close as they entered the Zwichen. The peace of the void was near and soon they would be home.

Then he could finally sleep.

They both could sleep.

ABOUT THE AUTHOR

Maggie Lynch is the author of 20+ published books, as well as numerous short stories and non-fiction articles. Her fiction tells stories of men and women making heroic choices one messy moment at a time. Her nonfiction focuses on helping indie authors be successful in their careers.

After careers in counseling, the software industry, academia, and worldwide educational consulting, Maggie chose to devote her time to her career as a full time author. Her fiction spans romance, suspense, fantasy and science fiction titles. Her non-fiction focuses on guiding authors to success in planning, distributing, and marketing their completed work.

facebook.com/maggiewrites

twitter.com/maggieauthor

instagram.com/mcvaylynch

amazon.com/author/maggielynchauthor

bookbub.com/authors/maggie-mcvay-lynch

pinterest.com/maggielynchauthor

Chameleon: The Choosing
Book 2 of The Forest People

Camryn approached the gateway tree with a combination of excitement and dread. Today she hoped to bond with a thunder dragon. But first she had to enter the lichen network and get to Arach Falls, the nesting grounds.

She had never been to Scotland, and outside of history studies had no idea what to expect of the Caledonian Forest. At least the tree network had this one mapped. Unlike the Eighre Terrace, where she rescued her father, this time she could travel in the fifth dimension. Dagger said it would be much easier than traveling in the eighth.

Yeah, right. Like having lichen crawling all over your body and down your throat was easy.

Camryn took a deep breath and backed against the gateway tree. She could see that accepting the lichen into her body was going to become a regular thing in this world. She'd just have to get used to it. *Arach Falls. Fifth Dimension. Arach Falls. Fifth Dimension.* The lichen pushed into her faster than before. She gasped her last breath as it filled her lungs and her world became a field of darkness dotted with points of light moving in all directions. She couldn't feel her body, but she felt the cold, and worse the nausea. Then a different tree spit her out.

The roaring of a large waterfall assailed her ears as she

uncurled from the wet lichen ball she had become. The lichen sloughed off Camryn's skin and furs, retreating into the flat rock beneath her, providing some cushion for her sore body. Now too hot and heavy, the furs clung to her in waterlogged stiffness. Grumbling, she pushed herself to sit and worked to remove the sodden strips from her legs and arms. She deposited them in a pile nearby. No use laying them out. There wasn't a dry spot in sight.

The tree at her back stood at a cave entrance where heavy mist covered every surface. Lichen grew on the underside of the cave and dripped water in bright green and orange rivulets. Along the ground it mounded over rocks and peeked in and out next to a stone pathway that ventured further into the darkness.

Having won the war with her stomach, Camryn stood carefully and turned in a slow circle, searching for any sign of Sela. Shielding her eyes against the sun, she watched as the sky darkened, and thunder and lightning heralded the arrival of the Sela and her blue dragon. Camryn scrambled beneath an outcropping at the cave's entrance. She did not want to be caught in those talons again, by accident or on purpose. The quicker she could get her own dragon the better.

Adalinda flapped her mighty wings once, twice and slowed into a smooth glide, descending in wide swooping circles, until she reached the ground and stepped forward on two powerful legs before settling about fifteen feet away and lowering her body to the ground.

Sela easily slid off Adalinda's back. Instead of the furs she'd worn on Eighre Terrace, Sela now wore grey, lightweight capris and a white tied blouse. Her white and grey tennis shoes were tied with pink laces. She patted Adalinda and nodded toward her, as if they were carrying on a conversation. After a few moments and another pat, Adalinda seemed to dissolve to nothing before Camryn's eyes.

"Whoa. I've never seen that before. Is that normal?" Camryn asked.

Sela giggled. They don't really need to fly to get to the Zwischen. But it's really hard on humans and most of the forest people to dissolve with them. When you travel the tree network, you are cocooned in lichen to protect you. When you fly a thunder dragon, when they fly high enough to create thunder, the lightning creates a protective bubble around you. Then you can go to the Zwischen, the void. But the dissolve doesn't allow them time to do that."

Camryn rubbed her fingertips in a circle motion to massage her forehead. So many things to learn in this world. Would she ever know everything she needed?

"I told her I needed to walk you into the nest and we would meet her inside," Sela said as she closed the gap between her and Camryn. "All those who go to the choosing must walk in the first time. I'm not sure why. I think it's some type of test. Ohar walked me in when I came and Adalinda chose me."

"So, if it weren't for me, you would normally fly in?"

"Not exactly fly. Just like the tree network, dragons travel inter-dimensionally. If I think of the nest, Adalinda takes me directly there. Once we reach the Zwischen, we dissolve from one place and appear in another."

"But no lichen, right? And what about the lights and the nausea?"

"Nausea?" Sela asked. No, I've never felt sick. It's just you start in one place, and in the blink of an eye you appear in another."

"You've never traveled the trees?"

"No." Sela frowned and the lines around her eyes crinkled.

"Agnoses are not allowed to travel the tree network. That's why having Adalinda is such a gift. It's the closest I can get to being a part of the lichen magic. It is a great gift that Ohar's mother sponsored for me. A great gift."

Camryn nodded, while also wondering if that meant Sela owed something to the Mazikeen queen. If Sela had to choose between Camryn and the queen, what would she do?

Camryn vowed to continue with caution. She really liked Sela and she wanted to trust her, but this was yet another reminder that everyone had loyalties and they weren't always open about the consequences of those loyalties.

Sela crossed in front of Camryn and pointed to stepping-stones leading to the interior of the cave. "This is where we start. The total drop of Arach Falls is over two hundred forty feet, but it is divided into three sections. We'll follow this path down to the river and then walk beside it until we come to the bridge at the first falls. We won't be able to talk until we get to the third section. The noise of the falls is too loud."

"What if we get separated?"

"That won't happen," Sela said. "There is only one way to get there. Once you start down the path it is almost impossible to turn and go back up. The best way out of the nest is with a dragon."

Camryn placed two fingers over her mouth. She wouldn't ask what happens if you are not chosen. She was the Chameleon, and according to everyone else, that was special. Surely she wouldn't be left without a dragon.

"There are a total of three chambers," Sela continued. "When we get to the final chamber we will have to swim beneath the falls."

"What?" Camryn shook her head. "I don't think so. We'd be killed by the power of the water. "

Sela must not have heard her, because she started down the path without looking back.

Camryn swallowed and hurried after her. How could anyone be ready to enter a nest of thunder dragons? She'd only ever seen three dragons, Sela's, Ohar's, and Dagger's. And Sela's was the only one she kind of met—if you called getting carried in its talons twice, and a couple of friendly pats to Adalinda's side, a meeting.

Following Sela down the first part of the path proved to be easier than it looked. Everywhere Camryn stepped, it seemed that dry lichen clung to the rock to provide a cushion and a little traction. Was it there before? She wasn't sure. The waterfall mist on her arms added to the shiver of misgiving working up her spine. There was nothing she could do about it now.

According to Dagger, bonding with a thunder dragon was the first step for her to be accepted by the Forest People. Although tales of the powers she used to rescue her father had traveled among many tribes, most still didn't trust her. She hadn't grown up with them. She didn't profess any loyalties to one tribe. But most of all she'd done absolutely nothing to change the mutations that were happening, driving some the People and animals deep into the darkness.

From the main cave she and Sela crossed a small bridge at the top of the falls. They then stepped gingerly, clinging to the cave wall as they descended to the pool below. Occasionally they were sheltered from the heavy mist of the falls by an overhang. Other times they were showered with water. The cold water made it more difficult to remain vigilant in choosing where to step since her entire body shook like a vibrating string.

At the bottom of the first falls, they crossed the river again jumping from stone to stone, and then climbed up to a ledge that led into a second chamber with stairs that wound like a corkscrew down a narrow, enclosed passageway. With no room to turn around and frequently having to duck as the space grew smaller, the deafening echo from the second falls stretched Camryn's nerves as taught as an overfilled balloon. Her shoulders tightened and reached toward her ears. Her stomach ached with dread.

As the ceiling became even lower, Camryn and Sela hunched at the waist. When they were forced to crawl on hands and knees, Camryn stopped and took several deep breaths, trying to ignore her spinning head and the unsteady bounce of Sela's light ahead of her. She blinked hard as her eyes swam and her head ached like a lightning strike with every beat of her heart.

I can do this. It can't be much farther.

She shuffled one hand ahead and then a knee, another hand, another knee, praying her ears wouldn't be permanently damaged by the time they finally got to the bottom.

Just as she thought she could stand it no longer, the tunnel turned away from the noise and she took a deep breath of gratitude. Few more feet of crawling and the tube expanded. The ceiling was now high enough they could finally stand again.

A brighter light beckoned at a larger opening ahead. Camryn emerged at a deep pool opposite a quiet trickle of falls. The shimmering, silver curtain cascaded over an expanse of rock equal to the wingspan of Sela's dragon. Dappled light entered the chamber from a shaft above.

Sela turned off her flashlight and stowed it in a belt around her waist. "This is where we swim," she said, her voice low, reverent. She stooped and tore off two pieces of blue-green lichen on a nearby stone. "Before you enter the water, put this over your nose and mouth. It will adhere and act like a rebreather for you. It extracts the oxygen from the water and allows you to breathe."

"Okay." Camryn drew out the word. Having traveled the tree network nine times now, this wasn't nearly as frightening as having lichen fill her lungs. "Will I be able to see you once we are in the water?"

"Yes, for the first part of our swim you will see everything clearly. There is no pollution at this level of the cave. This water is more pure than most drinking water."

Sela pointed toward the falls. "When we go under the falls, we will be swimming down a narrow tube for about a hundred feet before we emerge into the dragon's nest. There is no light inside the tube. So, after the first thirty feet or so it may be hard to see me ahead of you. But don't panic. Just keep moving forward. There are no branches off the tube, so you won't get lost.

"At about eighty feet you will see a small point of light at the end. Follow the light and you will exit at the pool next to the dragon's nest."

Camryn stiffened. She never liked it when someone said 'don't panic.' The fact they felt the need to say that generally meant there was good reason to panic. She'd heard that phrase from teachers during the short time she was in public school—teachers talking to the other students whenever Camryn became the freak. She'd heard that phrase too often at Starlight Center just before she was injected with a drug after making too many changes.

At least she controlled the changes now. She could maintain the visage she wanted at any time. The Kintala had done that for her.

"You ready?" Sela asked.

Camryn nodded. It didn't matter whether she was ready or not. She really didn't have a choice at this point.

Sela smoothed the lichen over her nose and mouth and Camryn did the same. It immediately adhered. She took a practice breath. Yes she could still breathe. She and Sela waded into the water. Sela gestured for Camryn to go under first. Camryn went further into the pool, and let it come over her head. Again, she took one, then two practice breaths. Cool! She could breathe perfectly.

Sela appeared next to her underwater. She raised her eyebrows and gave her the thumbs up sign, as if it were a question. Camryn nodded and also gave the thumbs up sign. Sela headed deeper in the water, her arms straight ahead and a dolphin kick propelling her downward.

Camryn swallowed her fear and concentrated on slowing her heart. *It's just like swimming in the lake on a camping trip*, she told herself. She was a good swimmer. Even when she'd been dumped from a raft on the Rogue River she'd made it to the bank without too much panic. *I can do this.* She dove into the water and chased after Sela.

Once her panic subsided, Camryn gloried in the ability to swim and breathe underwater. She fantasized about all kinds of swimming she could do in the future. She'd love to go to Hawaii and be able to swim with the fish without diving equipment. Or how about going in and out of old shipwrecks on the east coast? She'd read about some of those in National Geographic.

For just a moment she wondered if her adoptive mother knew about swimming with lichen. She wished she could have shared this with her? Did her mother ever want her own thunder dragon? For the first time she realized how much her mother gave up in order to spend the rest of her life with the man she loved—an Agnoses.

Camryn caught up to Sela treading water at the base of the falls. Though the falls were smaller than the other two they had traversed in the cave, she could still feel the power of the water. The sound was significantly more now than the sweet trickling she'd heard from the shore on the other side of the pool.

Sela faced her and made the sign for the tunnel and covered her eyes. When she removed her hand, she again raised her brows and put up a thumb as a question.

Camryn wanted to shake her head no. Dark tunnels were definitely not her thing. Instead she held up her thumb and nodded. She was almost there.

Just a hundred foot swim in a dark tunnel. How bad could that be? Others had done this before. Including Sela, she reminded herself.

Sela entered the tunnel first and Camryn swam directly behind her. It was only two or three kicks in and she could no longer see Sela ahead of her, but there was only one way to go. A small amount of light was still filtering from behind, so Camryn kicked again and continued forward. When complete darkness surrounded her, she tamped down on the automatic panic.

I knew this was coming. Just keep kicking.

She counted the kicks as she moved. Certainly by a hundred kicks she should be to at least the halfway point, maybe farther. Five, six, seven, eight…twenty-four, twenty-five, twenty-six.

Something slithered along her arms. What was that? Her heart rate increased. She kicked forward faster. Twenty-seven, twenty-eight, twenty-nine. Something slithered across her arm then across her cheek. No! Thirty. Her breaths came even faster. *Calm down!* Thirty-one. Thirty-two.

Sela didn't say there would be anything else in here, she reassured herself. *It's just your imagination playing tricks with your mind. Sela specifically said the water was pure, unpolluted. Surely she would have mentioned if there were other animals.*

Her panic set in deeper and her breaths were shallow. Though she couldn't see the tunnel sides she could feel them with her hands. Were they getting narrower? Would she get stuck?

Keep going. I can breathe through the lichen. Keep kicking. There is only one way. I can't get lost. I will see the light soon. Just keep going.

Fifty-two, fifty-three. Something slithered along her throat, then it wrapped around her several times and constricted. She reached up with her hands and pulled, but that only made it worse. She thrashed in the water. She pounded on the tunnel wall, hoping Sela—anyone—would hear and know that something was wrong.

"The Chameleon must die. Die now." The whispered voice bubbled through the water, with the words at the end of each sentence reverberating as she lost air...lost fight...lost everything.

For more books of the heart
Visit Windtree Press
http://windtreepress.com